straitjacket vacation

By Chris Sheehan

straitjacket vacation

By Chris Sheehan

First Published 2008

ISBN 978-0-557-00455-3

Copyright © 2008 Chris Sheehan

The moral rights of the author have been asserted. All rights reserved. No part of this publication may be reproduced, stored in a retrieval system or transmitted in any form or by any means, electronic, mechanical or otherwise without the written permission of the Publisher. Cover photo courtesy of Stephanie Roth.

To Maribel and Oscar

admittance

chapter one
admittance

"You're really going to enjoy the unit." the heavy-set nurse muttered in between almost obscene sounding deep breaths, "They'll be really nice to you there."

The stale scent of the spearmint chewing gum that she had obviously been chewing a few hours too long fills my nose each time she exhales. Making matters worse, is the fact that the stale gum smell is masking that of stale cigarettes.

She kneels down to be eye to eye with me, as I'm sitting on a tiny red stool meant for a small child, and

places her hands between her knees.

"They told me you haven't eaten in a few days."

Another wall of stale spearmint hits me; I do my best not to flinch.

"Is there anything I can get you to eat... a sandwich, perhaps?"

If there's one thing I hate, it's being spoken to as though I'm either a child or a fool... and so, I look up at her, as if to tell her to go fuck herself, and manage to mutter, "Yes, please."

And so, she leaves.

I examine my surroundings. I'm in a off-set room, with only three walls. There's a light blue curtain acting as the fourth. Against the far wall there's your generic computer equipment. Tempted to check out my file on the small monochrome monitor, but too fearful of getting caught. I am, after all, sitting in this room for a reason.

The left wall features all your standard medical charts. The anatomy of both genders, skeletal and musculature.

I stand and begin pacing between the left wall and the right. The right, filled with children's toys only made me feel even crazier than I originally had after being forced into the hospital. Old ragged stuffed-animals and barely garage-sale worthy Fisher Price type cheap plastic

furniture smeared with crayon and finger paint line the wall.

As I sit back down, I notice several clear drawstring sacks sitting on the examination table. Before I get the chance to check them out, I'm interrupted by a petite blonde holding a clipboard.

"Craig... Weiner is it?" she crinkled her nose. A somewhat attractive forty-something dressed completely in red, she proceeded over to a comfortable looking chair that I neglected to even notice was placed behind all the technical equipment.

She seemingly nestled herself into the chair, shifting herself ever so slightly to the left and right before settling in.

"Craig, how are we doing today?"

A therapy novice, though I may be, I hate the use of the word "we" as a way of softening one's independence when it comes to having problems like it somehow "lessens" the impact.

"I guess I've been better."

She didn't skip a beat.

"How so?"

For whatever reason, I instantly went on the defensive; tucking my chin to my chest... I couldn't come up with an actual response.

straitjacket vacation

"I can come back after you eat, if you'd like."

"No... It's okay. Just been a really bad day." I cracked my neck nervously, "Just never thought I'd get this far."

Lifting the tip of her pen to her lips, "Not many people do."

I nod.

Cocking her head to the side, "Though everyone had problems and challenges... it just takes certain strength to actually realize your need for and ask for help."

"I guess." I reply, furrowing my brow and scratching my head.

"So, tell me... what happened today?"

Leaning back on the child-size stool, almost to the point of falling over, I ready myself to tell my story.

"Well. I guess it all started falling about when I broke up with my long time fiancée--"

She interrupted, "That can be very traumatic. How long were you together?"

"About nine years" I reply, cracking my knuckles, which still bore the silver ring I wore on my left hand, that I used to convey that I was off-limits, "But, that's not really the end of it--"

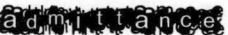

"What's that?" She cuts me off again.

"We had just bought a house together." I look down, "We're kind of stuck together, at least for a little while longer. Neither of us can afford this house on our own."

"Can I interrupt?" she interjected, raising her hand as if to tell me to slow down, "I spoke to your counselor at length earlier this afternoon, and we agree that your challenge is not with anything in specific, but with change at-large."

I shrug my shoulders.

"You've been tested for Bi-Polar, correct?"

"Yeah... a few times, actually."

"Okay, how about for anxiety?"

"I don't recall, but it wouldn't surprise me." I audibly sigh, "I think I've been tested for every head disease short of Alzheimer's."

She laughed.

"You don't look like you belong here."

Again, I shrug.

"You'll notice, if you make it to the unit... that not many of the folks there do."

straitjacket vacation

"Knock-Knock!" the original nurse barges in with two plastic enclosed sandwiches, cut diagonally, "I hope I'm not intruding."

My blonde doctor simply rolls her eyes, and excuses herself, so that I may eat in peace.

"Your mother is here to see you." the nurse mentions, as she draws back the curtain.

The curtain opens revealing my mother, as I'd never seen her before... openly weeping.

Our eyes meet, and she nearly collapses in grief.

"Ma, what's wrong?" I squirt the tiny mayonnaise packet onto my dry turkey sandwich.

"All of this is my fault!" she exclaims, "What have I done to you? This must have been something I've done!" she steadies herself on the examination table.

"Ma, this ain't your fault... and it's not necessarily a bad thing." I try to reassure her, my own eyes welling up.

She instantly takes notice of my hospital bracelet and gauzed-up inner elbow where I'd just recently had blood drawn, "Have they admitted you yet?"

"I don't know."

"How long are they going to keep you?"

"I don't know."

Tears began to flow heavily from my mothers blue eyes. As she was about to speak, the nurse barged in once more. "I hope we like Apple Juice!" she exclaimed, shaking two kid-size foil-topped apple juices.

I looked at her as if to tell her to fuck off; however, in an attempt to appear as sane as possible, I simply thanked her.

At this point, my mother was quite far gone in her grief. With a sarcastic smile and raised eyebrow, I offer her my second apple juice.

"Ya jerk!" my mother laughed through her tears.

The blonde doctor peeked her head through the curtain, "I'm afraid we need to cut this visit short." drawing the curtain open, "You may wait outside until we decide whether or not we need to keep Craig overnight."

My mother grabs me and hugs me as if she thought she'd never see me again. Though long and tight, the hug felt quite empty.

The doctor closes the curtain behind my mother, and returns to the comfortable looking chair. The seat must have maintained her imprint, as there was far less nestling this time.

"Are you feeling better since you've eaten?"

I raise an eyebrow, as if to ask "Are you serious?"

straitjacket vacation

I was, after all, still chewing the food.

"How long has it been since you've eaten?"

I take a second to swallow my food, "Since I moved into the new house, I guess."

"... and that was?"

"About a week ago…"

"Okay… and no hunger pangs?"

"None."

"Okay." she clears her throat, as if to shift into autopilot, "It appears as though we're entering a pretty severe depression."

Scribbling away on her clipboard, she asks "Have you lost interest in things that once brought you great joy?"

"Yeah... I already checked-off that box on my depression survey. Didn't my counselor give that to you?"

Crinkling her nose, "Ya know, I'm pretty sure she did. I'd like to re-index you, though, if you don't mind."

I shrug.

"I take that as a yes?"

I nod.

admittance

"Have you put any thought into hurting yourself or anybody else?"

I shake my head.

"So..." her eyes burn a hole in mine, "No thoughts of suicide?"

"No."

She gives me an incredulous look, while flipping through my file. She stops on a page, and begins to read in a robotic monotone, "I just feel trapped. I'm looking for any way out."

I raise an eyebrow.

"These were your words to your counselor earlier this afternoon." she underlines the quote on the clipboard, "People who are looking for 'a way out'..." she said, with air-quotes, "... are people we take very seriously, and would like to see receive help."

We stare at each other in silence for what feels like an hour. She finally spoke, "I'm going to recommend for you to stay here for a day or two... if that's okay?"

"Can I leave whenever I want?"

She laughed, "Of course you can. This isn't prison."

"I'll go and get all of the forms you'll need to sign off on, a well as your Patient's Bill of Rights." abruptly, she left the room, as though I was an afterthought.

straitjacket vacation

"Can I see my mother? Just want to fill her in on what's going on so she doesn't wind up in here herself."

"Of course." She laughed, "Only briefly, though." She tied off the curtain, so that it remained open, "We will have to fit you for a gown, and check you for scars."

I plop down on the stool, awaiting my mother's arrival, so I can bid her good night. I take note of the irony of the hospital leaving several drawstring plastic sacks in the same room as a man who's currently been deemed "potentially suicidal". I chuckle to myself, and think of the humor that would be involved, if I so decided to asphyxiate myself right here in the behavioral health ward. Ultimately, I decide against it... after all, if I'm dead, I won't be able to tell the story.

My mother returns to my makeshift room after having calmed herself down a great deal.

"They're keeping you overnight."

"Yeah."

"Are you scared?" she puts her hand on my shoulder.

"Nah... I think I'll be okay. After all, it's only overnight."

"Have you called Danielle?"

"Not yet... That, I'm a bit scared of."

"How about in to work?"

"No.", it's beginning to set in that I'm going to be unable to return home tonight. I stifle a slight panic attack. My breathing becomes heavier; however, I'm hesitant to let my mother see me become upset.

"Is there anything you're going to need?" my mother inquires, "Extra clothes, or anything?"

"I guess I'll need something to sleep in." I reply, "... and something to read. I don't want to actually have to converse with any of these people."

"Craig!" my mother pleads, "You need to take full advantage of your time here!"

She continues, "This needs to be a learning experience. Part of your problem is that you keep too yourself too much."

"So... you gonna bring me a book or not?" I laugh.

My mother rolls her eyes.

"Man of Steel, by John Byrne... it should be in one of the book boxes in the garage,"

"I'll have your brother look for it" she sighs, "At the desk, they told me we can see you one hour a day for visitation. Six o'clock in the evening."

"Well, hopefully by that time tomorrow, I'll be ready to come home."

straitjacket vacation

"You've just got to try your best, and follow the doctor's advice. Don't turn this into a waste of time." she states firmly.

I nod.

The nurse wobbles back in, a stack of papers about an inch thick in her hand, and a light blue gown draped over her arm. "Time to say good night!" she says, slapping the papers down on the examination table, "You can see Craig tomorrow, after supper."

"You'll need to empty your pockets." she continues, "We'll keep your belongings safe, here."

I snicker, and decide to give my mother the contents of my pockets, my wallet, keys and cellular phone. I kiss my mother goodbye as the nurse hands me my gown.

"This is a special gown. For the behavioral health Unit." she grabs at the arm hole of the gown, "No strings!" she chuckles. "I can help you put it on, if you'd like."

Dodging a waft of foul breath, I shake my head, "I'm quite sure I can figure this out."

Almost insulted, she retorts, "I'll need your tie, belt and shoes before I can leave the room."

I oblige, once more noting the irony, that they allowed me to wear my tie and belt for this long.

She proceeds to haphazardly "fold" my tie and belt,

and place them into one of the clear plastic draw-string sacks. After writing my name on the sack, she tosses my shoes in for good measure, pretty much undoing any "folding" she may have had done.

"I'm going to leave this bag in here with you." cocking her head in the direction of a second plastic sack, "Undress, and place all of your clothes in there."

She leaves the room, this time affixing a hook from the wall onto the curtain to ensure my privacy.

I begin to undress. With every button on my shirt that I undo, I feel more and more like a caged animal.

I begin to experience something that I can only describe as heartburn's cold cousin, rising and submerging from my stomach to the back of my throat. I feel like I need to use the bathroom, and remember my fear of using public toilets... I sit down, as I figure it was the best alternative to passing out.

"Have to keep it together!" I tell myself, "These people already think I'm crazy. I need to calm down!"

At this point, I'm shirt less. I poke my head out from the curtain. "Nurse?"

Nobody even looks in my direction.

"Nurse???"

Finally, a rotund black male nurse happens by. Reeking of Old Spice and baring a gap between his teeth

straitjacket vacation

that I could probably fit my thumb through, he asks condescendingly, "What can I do for you, young man?"

"I need my nurse!"

"Ho'kay, we need to sit down faw a second and calm down" his voice squeaks, "Everything will be okay."

"Listen, man." I tremble, "This is... was, a big mistake... I gotta get outta here, I gotta go home!"

"Son--"

I cut him off, "I've got work in the morning."

He laughs, "No you don't. Only work you gots in the mawnin' is on yo'self."

I sit on the floor, "How long are they going to keep me here?"

"I wouldn't know, young man. Ever'body's different."

"What's the average length of stay here?"

"Son, I can't say." he scratches his bald head, "Some people stay faw a few hours... some, a few days... others, a few weeks."

"Weeks?" I exclaim.

"I'm shaw you won't be here that long."

I begin to take off my socks.

"Lemme get you some hospital booties, young man." he smiled, full gap exposed, "You just never know what's been on these floors."

I quickly pull my socks back on.

He laughs, "I'll be right back, boy. Don'tcha worry 'bout nothin'... ever'thin's gonna be okay."

I stand up, and examine the gown. It looks to be fitted to about my height, but looks as though it could wrap around me at least a half-dozen times. I hated to admit, that I may not be able to figure this one out.

I attempt to finagle the gown around myself several times before the male nurse returned.

Giggling like a child, he doubled over, hands to his knees... dropping the 'hospital booties' in the process, "Boy, lemme help ya with that."

Placing his hand on my shoulder to steady me, he slips my right arm into the arm hole, turns me around twice, and then puts my right arm through a second arm hole. Wrapped like a burrito with arms, I stand mortified. Just twelve hours ago, I was running one of the largest paper producing companies in town, and now, I'm in a sleeveless straitjacket.

"Alright, young man... we can lose the pants and draws now." still smiling his gappy grin, "I'll leave ya be, child. You need anything else, I be over there." he motions to the nurse's station.

straitjacket vacation

I nod.

I feel the cool gown on my back. The coolness extends down my legs as I remove my pants. I feel dirty. Like sleeping on sheets that you know someone's recently relieved themselves on. Imaginary or not, the pungent aroma of urine wafted into my nostrils, almost burning with each inhale.

I sit back down on the floor, to change into the hospital booties, which the nurse had neglected to pick back up after dropping them. They were stiff, and smelled like old corn-chips. The white "grip tape" on the soles were now a dull gray and for the most part peeled off, indicating many wears before my own. The thought of asking for a newer pair goes through my mind, however, I decide the least burden I am on these people, the saner they may think I am... and ultimately, the sooner I get to go home.

My original nurse, fresh off a cigarette break, returns to the room. "I see we're in our hospital outfit", she remarks, "Let's go over these forms real quick."

She rolls a stool into my room, and plops onto it. In her hand there's a clipboard, with the inch-thick stack of papers. I take notice of the fact, that this time; she didn't even have the decency to chew a stick of gum after her last drag.

After about an hour, we get through all the paperwork, including a so-called "Patients-Bill-of-Rights", which told me, I was free to do as I pleased, however, anything I did that went against "their orders" would be

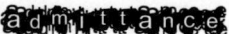

grounds to end my insurance coverage.

"So... I really don't have much of a choice in when I can leave." I note.

"Honey, you've been admitted. It's in the doctor's hands now." she places her hand on my knee, "Just do as they tell you, and you'll be out of here in no time."

A younger nurse enters the room, "Knock-Knock!" she sings, "Are we ready for the scar check yet?" This nurse; actually a nurse in training, was in her early twenties. She had shoulder length brown hair with blonde streaks scattered throughout. She was of Hispanic descent, and had the second darkest brown eyes I'd ever seen, next to my ex-fiancée Danielle. Her face was gorgeous, though, her scrubs made it difficult to make out her body shape. She appeared to be quite petite.

"Oh, that's right!" the first nurse exclaims, sticking her index finger up, "We need to photograph you."

"Okay." I shrug, "Do I need to stand?"

"Actually", the young nurse chimed, "You'll need to stand... and strip."

"What?"

"I'm sorry, Craig." the new nurse said, re-affixing the hook to the curtain.

With that, I stand up. I extend my arms out, resembling the Vitruvian Man, and get unwrapped. I stand

straitjacket vacation

there, in all my glory for about thirty seconds. That's how long it took them to realize they'd need to retrieve a camera before taking any pictures.

"Shit." the young nurse slaps her forehead, "I'm sorry, where's the camera?"

"At the station!" my original nurse hollered, "Go get it!"

The gown is tossed over me, as the young nurse heads out for the camera. I cling to it; to make sure I'm as covered as possible.

An eternity later, the young nurse returns with a five-hundred year old Polaroid camera. "Okay, Craig... we'll get this right yet!"

The old nurse excuses herself to "process my paperwork", while I get ready for my "close-up".

Upset, I throw the gown over to the examination table and extend my arms out.

Like fucking Federico Fellini, this new nurse starts circling me with the camera. I was halfway expecting her to ask me to "work it".

SNAP - There's one of my face

SNAP - There's one of my neck

SNAP - There's one of my chest and stomach

SNAP – There's one of my waist and crotch

SNAP – There's one of my legs

SNAP – There's one of me ankles and feet

SNAP – There's one of my forearms and wrists

SNAP, SNAP, SNAP, SNAP – She's behind me now, and I can almost feel the heat of the flash going off on my backside with each click.

"So… um, why so many of my ass?" I ask.

"We just need to make sure there's nothing up there."

"You're not serious?"

"Afraid so..." with some trepidation in her voice, "I'm going to need you to, um... shift."

My head sinks into my shoulders, and I grab my privates and hold them over to one side, "How's this?"

Before she can answer, my original nurse throws open the curtain, "All done?" she sings.

"Are you fucking kidding me?" I exclaim, as I stand in all my glory, with a handful of genitalia in full view of the entire nurse's station.

"Oh my God." she pulls the curtain over, "I'm so sorry, Mr. Weiner."

straitjacket vacation

She tosses me my gown, which, this time I'm actually able to successfully wrap myself in, "Please, have a seat. We've requested someone from The Unit to escort you up. Should only be a few minutes."

I nod.

"They'll be bringing a wheelchair for you to sit in."

"I think I'll be fine to walk." I reply.

"Sorry, Craig." the nurse retorts, waving her portly finger in my face, "Insurance policy here at the hospital reads that when a patient is admitted, they go by wheelchair."

She kneels down to my eye level once more, "… and besides, The Unit's allllll the way on the other side of the complex. You don't want to walk all that way, do you?"

I roll my eyes, as the nurse slowly backs herself out of my room. This time she leaves the curtain fully open.

It's nearing midnight, and the nursing shift begins its change. I watch the second shift and third shift share their stories, and pass along their information. They share phony smiles, and even phonier greetings. I hear the third shift complain about the way the second shift left the break room. I hear the second shift refer to the third shift as "The Mutants".

I sit in the midst of this sudden rush of hustle and bustle, and feel as though the immediate few feet around me is moving in extreme slow motion.

The "few minutes" I'm told to wait turns into a few hours. I take the time to reflect on exactly how I wound up in my current situation.

* * * * *

This was supposed to be the greatest week of my life. The culmination of so many things, such hard work and an incredibly large dose of luck all rolled into one.

Tonight is the second of August.

All the things I had one during the first half of the year were supposed to pay off this month.

Since about April, my fiancée, Danielle, and I have been trying to buy our first home together...

I appear to be getting ahead of myself.

In early March of this year, Danielle and I celebrated our nine year anniversary. We'd been through a lot in our time together, including bouts of alleged infidelity and seeming disinterest in one another, the bouts would come and go... sometimes, often, other times more sporadic, and I figured it was normal.

During our second year together, we bought each other "promise rings". They were nothing too fancy or expensive, just your basic sterling silver bands that you'd find at any Mall's silver kiosk. We never really considered ourselves "engaged" per say, however, we always seemed to see marriage as all but a foregone conclusion.

Several years later, she lost hers.

For this anniversary, I decided to buy her another silver "promise" band. I placed it in a slice of her favorite strawberry shortcake, and laughed when she almost ate it. It was that night that we realized our love would be forever. Life simply couldn't happen or continue any other way. Or, so we thought.

That weekend, she asked me if I'd be willing to buy a house with her. I kind of shrugged it off, as I really wasn't making too much money (I could barely afford my studio apartment), and was almost literally drowning in debt.

I relented, and accompanied her to see some model homes that were being built several miles south of town. What started off as a chore, turned into a rather pleasant morning. We stopped for breakfast at a local fast food restaurant. As we were leaving, she asked, "So, where are we going on our honeymoon?"

I gave a double-take, and laughed, "What are you talking about?"

She coyly smiled, and I noticed her playing with her new ring. This ring obviously represented a lot more than the first one.

"I dunno..." I shrug, "Where do you wanna go?"

"I was thinking something exotic... and different." she tapped on her bottom lip with her left index finger,

"How about Tokyo?"

"Tokyo?" I exclaim, "That sounds like a blast!"

For the next several weeks, I proudly announced to everyone that would listen that I was going to be getting married.

I received plenty of congratulations, but, at the same time, a lot of raised eyebrows. Our relationship, after all, was always a bit on the rocky side… and I suppose I wasn't always that "tight-lipped" about it.

From here, we decided to purchase a home. We knew that neither of us could qualify for a home loan on our own, so we went down to the bank together.

Much to our surprise, we were informed we would be approved for a home worth up to a half million dollars. Danielle's eyes widened, and looked in my direction. I laughed it off, and informed her we'd be in the market for something just a bit more conservative.

From April to July, every evening after work, we pounded the pavement with our Real Estate Agent, who also happened to be my mother. We couldn't agree on anything, and the things we did agree on, were far out of our price range. On top of all of this, time and time again, I found myself caught in between my mother and Danielle... who, for whatever reason, didn't want to communicate with each other. Using me as a go-between, I had to deal with the brunt of both of them.

By this point, I'd already given my notice to the

straitjacket vacation

apartment complex I was staying at. Time was definitely against us.

It came down to three houses.

One was a newer model, but incredibly small. The other two were a bit older, and were quite a bit larger. They were priced comparably, and were all in nice neighborhoods.

Danielle instantly fell in love with the smaller home, while I maintained we should try to get the most space for our money.

Danielle, being Danielle, got her way. I would've done just about anything for her, including give up precious square-footage for her happiness and comfort.

We sent in a fair offer, which was immediately rejected. Rather than pay more than the house was worth, or jump through several flaming hoops, we decided to move on to one of the larger homes.

At this point, one of the larger homes had already sold. Leaving us with only one option... which would be the home we would finally purchase.

The final half of the month of July was a blur of paperwork, walkthroughs, and inspections. All the while, I was still putting in near ten hour days at the office. As our closing date drew ever closer, I began to leave the office earlier and earlier each day.

I was called into my Manager's office two days prior

to closing. To my surprise, he was joined by the Vice-President of the company.

"Craiger!" the Vice-President exclaimed, "I hear you're on your way to becoming a real grown up?"

I smiled.

"Gettin' married!" he gives me a light punch on the shoulder, "Buyin' a house!"

Still smiling, I nervously scratched my head.

"Gettin' promoted to Paper Plant Supervisor!" he winks.

"Huh?"

"Congratulations, Mr. Weiner." he smiles, "Or should I say, Supervisor Weiner?"

"Sir, thank you!"

"Oh, no... Thank you." he handed me a gift card to a local restaurant, "All your hard work hasn't gone unnoticed."

As I turned to leave the room, I was informed that with my new position, I wouldn't be able to take the following week off to move into my new home.

I wanted to complain, but I simply nodded.

Closing on the house came and went without a hitch.

straitjacket vacation

It was a Friday afternoon. I spent the entire weekend moving all of my belongings in. Sunday night would be our first night staying over at the new home.

Laying in bed next to Danielle. The ceiling fan above us going at medium speed, the binds lazily swaying in the semi-regular breeze. Everything seemed perfect.

New House.

Promotion at Work.

Engaged to be Married.

Perfect!

Danielle turned to me, "Can you get me some water?"

I got out of bed and proceeded down the hallway to the kitchen. It's at this moment that I realize just how tremendous this house is as compared to my tiny studio apartment. I felt a bit of a panic, realizing the amount of responsibility I now had. "At least I've got Danielle." I tell myself.

Standing at the sink, getting Danielle her drink, I peered out the kitchen window to see the half-acre of grass and rock that I now owned. A bit more panic rose up my throat. "At least I'm not alone." I assure myself.

I headed back down the hallway towards the master bedroom. I passed the other three bedrooms that we hadn't yet figured out uses for. All I knew was that I was going to paint one of them pink for Danielle the following

weekend so that she could have her own office space.

As I'm about to enter the master bedroom, I heard some whimpering. I found Danielle sobbing uncontrollably.

Almost dropping the glass of water, I fell to my knees to see what was wrong.

"This was all a big mistake!" she cried, "I can't live here with you!"

"What?" I panic, "What are you talking about?"

"This just isn't right. I need to go home."

I tried to settle her down. I tried to hug her, only to get pushed away.

"I'm going home!" she shrieked.

I lost my balance, having been settled on the balls of my feet, and plopped down on my backside, water splashing on my left shoulder. She began to get dressed, and without any further explanation, she left.

I heard the heavy front door slam behind her, and began to wonder just what I had gotten myself into. Just that morning, I'd woken up in my tiny apartment, totally excited for my future. Here I sat, on the floor of this new alien room, in this new alien house… alone.

I sat there the remainder of the night, not moving or sleeping at all. My alarm went off at six in the morning. It beeped for nearly two hours before I got up.

straitjacket vacation

I called Danielle. No answer.

I called my mother. She was in a meeting.

I called into work. I was told that I was expected for a presentation an hour ago, and that I had best get in if I wanted to keep my job.

I crawled over to the bathroom, and did my best to freshen myself up. I kind of brushed my teeth, and kind of ran a comb through my hair. I did my best to shave a bit. I knew, in the end it wouldn't matter... as I felt like absolute dog shit.

I managed to arrive at work, to find several employees talking about my absence during the morning's presentation. I hobbled over to my good friend, Robert, to find out what I'd missed.

"Craig, what the fuck happened to you, man?"

"Nothin' man, just a bad night."

"Dude, why don't you just head home for the day...? I'll cover for you."

"There's nothing for me at home... I'll try to hang out here as long as I can."

The day felt as though it lasted a month. I just sat in my office, facing the wall... occasionally rocking back and forth in my chair. Two of our warehouse workers, who we endearingly referred to as "The Creep" and "Scum Bag"

took notice of my demeanor, and tried to cheer me up several times throughout the day... at least that's what they told me. I was way too far gone in thought to even realize.

Robert did whatever he could to deflect any work from hitting my desk. Not that it would have mattered anyway. I was seeing white the entire day. Couldn't read the simplest text, couldn't decipher the simplest shapes. I really felt as though I was on the brink of losing my mind.

I vaguely remember thinking about running away. Stuffing my little car with whatever I could carry, and whatever meant enough to me to keep... and just driving away. Either until I found somewhere to be or wherever I ran out of gas and money. Then I would just live, or die. I made several attempted excursions to my car that afternoon, each time getting a little closer than the last. I wanted to go away so badly.

I felt like a failure. I'd wasted the past nine years of my life with a woman who doesn't think she can ever live with me. I invested a quarter of a million dollars in a home to share with this same woman. A home, which I couldn't stay in... Not comfortably, anyway. A home, which I could never even hope to afford on my own.

The whole year's work, for all of my bravado and big-talk, was, at this point swirling ever so quickly down the toilet. I wanted to vomit, yet there was nothing in my stomach.

There was a knock on my office door. It was Robert, "Dude, you plan on staying all night?" the clock on the

straitjacket vacation

wall read seven o'clock, "Ya can't avoid the house forever, man."

He was right.

I packed up my things, and drove back to the house, where I sat in darkness until morning falling asleep at odd intervals.

I called my mother to inquire about placing the house back on the market. She told me it was a terrible idea, and that this would all just blow over. She knows how lousy I am when it comes to adjusting, and simply took this as another instance of my maladjustment. She told me to keep the house for a month, and then we would revisit the notion of selling.

This was yesterday.

This morning started with an alarm going off. This was a different kind of alarm that I was accustomed to. My phone was ringing. It was Danielle.

"You told your Mother that I wouldn't live with you???" she screamed, "I just got off the phone with your mother, and she asked me what my problem was."

"Wha?" I stammer trying to rub the sleep out of my eyes.

"Forget it. Forget everything!" still screaming, "We're through. We're done. I'm done!"

"Babe? What are you talking about?"

"You figure out what to do with that fucking house. I'm done." her voice began to crack, "The house can fucking foreclose for all I care!"

"We really need to talk this out."

"Forget it, I'm done talking!"

"Babe--"

She cut me off, "You're late for work! You better get going if you want to keep affording your house!"

She then hung up, and I launched the phone across the room.

Composing myself, I crawled back into the bathroom, much like I did the day before... this time hurling my limp and numb body into the shower, where I laid on the floor for the next hour. Fifteen minutes in, the water turned from warm to a brisk and bitter cold... I still laid there, shivering. Trying to cover myself with myself.

There was a knock at my door.

I crawled out of the shower, which was still running... wrapped myself in whatever I could find as I approached the door.

It was my younger brother, Anthony.

"Craig, man... Mom wanted me to check to see if you were okay. Danielle just called her."

straitjacket vacation

"Nah, man. I'm fine." I lied, "Just not feeling too well."

I was always hesitant to show weakness around Anthony. In many ways, I was the only "father figure" or "male-role model" he'd ever had. At least that's how I saw things. I always wanted him to see me as strong, and someone he could rely on, should the need arise. It absolutely killed me to stand here, in front of him, completely broken.

The look in his eyes told me immediately that he knew I was lying. I looked down, sheepishly... "Shit, man... uh, I'd better get back into the shower before I lose all the hot water."

"Okay, man." he tried to get a better look in my eyes, "Call me if you need anything."

"Yeah, cool... man, thanks." I sigh, realizing I may have put one over on him.

As he walked across my grass to his car, he turned back, "and, call Mom!"

Fuck.

I did my best to finish showering, and do all my normal hygiene routine... My cell phone tells me I've missed eight calls… all from my mother.

I headed out to the car, and called my mother as I headed to work. Today, I found myself nearly four hours

admittance

late.

I was upset that she'd taken it upon herself to call Danielle, and made sure she knew it. I told her that I'd felt as though my life was falling apart, and I had no more control.

She had asked when my next therapy session was... and I wasn't sure. She advised me to call my counselor and request an appointment later that afternoon. I told her I'd think about it, but I was sure I wouldn't need it.

Forty-five minutes later, I tried to sneak into my office. I found Robert sitting behind my desk, "Dude, the morning's paperwork is all taken care of." he remarked, "There's a fresh pot of coffee in the back too."

I looked down and shook my head, smiling, "Thanks, man. You're a life saver."

I headed to the break room, and poured myself some coffee. The Creep approached.

"Hey, Craig" he asked, "Is everything cool? You're not mad at me are you?"

I gave him a half-smile, fully realizing that given his limited mental capacity that he takes everything so personally. "Nah, man... we're cool. I'm just having problems at home."

He repeatedly nods his head, as though he were part chicken. His dirty hair shook particles of dust into the air each time. He smiles, baring a mouthful of teeth that would make a shark jealous. His sheer naïveté puts a full smile on my face, almost a giggle. I pat him on the shoulder of the filthy football jersey he was wearing. Using his real name for the first time in ages, I mutter "Thanks, Joey."

He immediately stops nodding, as if his power cord had just been pulled... cocked his head to the side, and asked, "For what?"

Patting him on the shoulder again, "Don't worry about it, Joey. Don't worry about it."

I headed down the hallway towards my office, sipping my coffee. The Scum Bag leapt out in front of me. "Shit man, what da fuck? You ain't gonna say hello?"

"Hey, what's up, Scum Bag"

"Shiiit, man! Where da fuck you been?" he yanked on his ear, "You fuckin' around wit' some shit, or somethin'?"

"Nah." I scratched my head.

"Di'nt you jus' buy a house or somet'ing?" he yanked at the front of his pants, "You can't be affordin' to cut out'a work, mang!"

"Yeah, dude... I know... I'll check you out later."

I excused myself, and happened to notice the office we'd kept empty of late, part office part conference room... I was drawn in by the light that peered through its window. This office was painted a bit differently than the

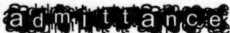

rest of the building, making the light appear brighter. I entered the empty office, and sat in one of the many rolling chairs that inhabited it.

I wheeled myself over to the window, and stared. The light was nearly blinding, but I could still make out what was outside. I got a sudden burst of energy, and dizzily stood up.

I wandered into my office, using the chair rail on the wall as a guide, "Rob... I... I'm gonna head out."

"Goin' home? Good man, take a load off."

"Nah, bro... just goin' for a ride... I'll be back in a bit." I steadied myself against the wall, feeling almost drunk.

"Are you sure?" Robert began to stand up.

I motioned for him to sit back down, "Nah, man... I'll be okay. Just need to clear my head."

Robert sat back down, "Okay, Craig. Be careful, man."

I headed for the parking lot.

"Call if you need anything!"

I waved as I headed towards the car. Unaware where I was headed, I stopped halfway through the parking lot. I looked down, and remember being vaguely impressed at the fact that my clothing matched. I coughed a slight laugh,

straitjacket vacation

and continued to the car.

    I stood at the car door for a few moments, worried that my friends and family were worried about me. I contemplated heading back to the office, but really felt a change of environment would help me out at that point in time.

    I opened the car door, and felt the brick-oven-quality burst of heat that had built up inside on this incredibly hot summer day. Wincing a bit, I proceeded to sit down. I decided to drive downtown. To a neighborhood I used to work in. A familiar neighborhood, with familiar sights, and if I were lucky, familiar people.

    I knew the Expressway would get me to my destination too fast, so I decided to take the side streets. Crammed full of your assorted filth and trash, were these side streets. Taking note of the low-end gang members, and low-rent prostitutes... I began to realize my life may not be as bad as I'd previously believed.

    I continued past a few fast food restaurants I'd frequented just days earlier. I remember wishing I could just "go back" to the last time I was there. I could almost picture myself eating at the nearby Fish 'n Chips shack the week prior. Happy as a clam, engaged to be married and moving into my very first home.

    If I only knew then...

    I passed the Veteran's Memorial Cemetery, and almost felt envious of the folks currently six feet below the street level. I remember being terribly ashamed thinking

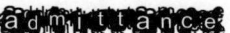

that almost immediately. I carried on.

My phone began to ring. It was my mother.

I turned down the volume on Rush Limbaugh, and answered the phone.

"Where are you?"

"Driving."

"You're not at work?"

"No."

"Where are you going?"

"Not sure."

"Are you going to go to work?"

"Not sure."

"You need to get in to see your counselor today."

"No, I don't.", I hung up the phone.

I crossed the expressway overpass, and traffic came to a screeching halt. Downtown traffic is usually pretty bad, however, due to excess construction today's was incredibly intense. This was traffic that you almost had to want to be in. Having nowhere in particular to be, I happily joined the queue.

straitjacket vacation

I noticed the downtown hustle and bustle, and instantly began to feel envious. These were people who had places to be, and reasons for being there. Most probably had homes and families. Both to support and to share their lives with. I almost lose myself in their lives. Wanting so bad for mine to have the same meaning and depth.

I tapped on the brakes.

Fucking construction.

I tapped the gas pedal. We moved nearly a car length.

I grew impatient, and turned into a motel parking lot. This was where everything start to get cloudy.

The next thing I knew, my phone was ringing.

I found myself standing in the middle of what appeared to be a second hand store. People were walking past me, nudging me out of their way. I swayed with the foot traffic until I fully came to. The almost thick aroma of people's used belongings filled my nose, the sound of thick Spanish accents filled my ears.

I answered my phone, without even checking to see who it was.

It was my mother, again.

"Where are you?"

"I..." I shook my head, "I don't know."

"What?"

"I'm... I'm not sure." I began to panic.

"Are you okay?"

"I... I think so, I..."

"I'm going to call your counselor."

"Uhm... okay. Cool. Uhh, I... I... gotta go." I hung up, almost dropping my phone.

I look around, and see used clothing all around me. The acrid smell of mothballs burnt my nostrils. I stumble a bit, catching myself of a rack full of old electronics. Record players, VCR's, VCR Rewinders, cloudy clear plastic tote after plastic tote full of multi-colored sticky looking smelly wires.

I regained my balance, and felt around my pockets. I quickly came to the realization that I no longer had my car keys. My heart beating out of my chest, I felt like scratching my way through the walls to get out.

I tried to work my way towards what I thought would be the "front" of this store, and found myself in an "Employees Only" area. This store was horse-shoe shaped, so I was actually in the exact opposite location than I wanted to be.

After what felt like a half hour, I made it to the exit. I tried to ask where I was, however my High School

straitjacket vacation

level Spanish wasn't good enough to make any meaningful or helpful conversation.

I stumbled into the parking lot, and surveyed for my car. I didn't see it.

I follow the building around to its rear, and plopped down on the curb.

I sat there for a minute... with my head in my hands.

I didn't know where I was.

I didn't know where my car was.

I didn't know where my keys were.

I was, in a word, lost. For the first time in my life, I was absolutely lost.

I pulled myself back up; using one of the consignment store's shopping carts for balance. I peered across a small alley that was between the store and a small Korean church, only to find my car.

I ran over to my car, not only to find it in perfect condition, but with my keys in the ignition. Relieved, I hopped in the car. There wasn't as big of a blast of heat when I opened the door, which told me I hadn't been where ever I was for very long.

I turned on the car, and checked the clock. I'd been away from the office nearly four hours. Of which, I could only consciously remember one.

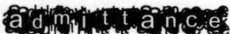

Pulling back into traffic, I was unsure of where I was. Having only a vague idea, I headed back in what I thought was the direction back to my office.

I remembered a few nights prior promising to pick up a depilatory cream for Danielle, as she had a gynecologist appointment this afternoon, and wanted to ensure her legs would be bare. I found the nearest drug store, and picked up a can.

Twenty minutes later, I found myself not in front of my office, but hers. I placed the thin can of cream on her driver's side tire, as not to interrupt her day. A quick text message later, and she knew that I'd been there.

Tempted to see her to exit the building, I wanted to wait. I thought better of it, and drove on.

Seemingly in complete control of my faculties once more, I made it back to work.

Robert met me at the front door, "Dude, your mom's been calling. You got a doctor's appointment in like fifteen minutes."

"What?" I pulled my phone out of my pocket, "She never told me."

"Man... you just gotta go." he shrugged, "Just take it easy, man. Everything's gonna be okay."

"Alright, I'll run the reports and go--"

straitjacket vacation

"Craig, the reports are done, man. You just gotta go."

I relented, as I couldn't think of any other excuse to stay.

"Call if you need anything, man." he waved, "I mean it, man. ANYthing!"

I nodded, and looked down, ashamed that I seemingly couldn't handle life at the moment.

Loading myself back into the car, I headed towards my counselor's office.

My counselor was a nice older woman. Someone I fully trusted, and felt I can confide just about anything in. At the risk of sounding "Florence Nightingale-esque", I really thought she cared about my problems, and would like to see me succeed in life. I felt awful for her having to make a special trip to the office to see me. I really hate putting people out like that.

I arrived at her office about five minutes late for my appointment, to find her sitting in the waiting room. She had a stern stiff-lipped look on her face, almost annoyed. Her legs were crossed. She was reading a magazine.

"Craig!"

"I'm so sor--", she cut me off.

"Why didn't you call me?" she put down the magazine,

"I told you, that if you needed to talk whenEVER, you were to call me!"

I shrugged and struggled to speak. Nothing came out.

"Okay, okay... let's go into the office." She smiled, and put her arm around my shoulders.

We approached her office, and I felt a welling in my throat. I hadn't felt like that since I was a child. She guided me over to the usual chair I'd sit in during our sessions, and asked "Now, Craig... What's wrong?"

... And just like that.

I exploded.

My eyes erupted in a way that they hadn't in nearly twenty years. I bawled like a baby.

She excused herself for a moment, and returned with a box of tissues.

"Jesus Christ, ain't I a cliché?" I laughed.

"Oh, Craig." she smiled, "Tell me what's troubling you."

"Didn't my mother--"

"Your mother isn't who I drove all the way out here for." she sternly wagged her finger, "You are. Tell me what's troubling you."

straitjacket vacation

Trying to compose myself, all I could do is apologize for inconveniencing her.

"I'm going to slap you if you don't stop that." she joked, "This is serious. Tell me what's the matter."

I related the story of my past couple of days, losing control of my emotions several times along the way. I noticed she didn't have her clipboard or my file this time, which both relieved me and worried me at the same time.

During my seemingly unstoppable ramble, she stopped me, "Have you thought about hurting yourself?"

There it was.

There was the question I'd been fearing I'd be asked. Not so much because I was suicidal or anything, I just found it to be such a demeaning question. A question that's only gets asked to folks that have hit absolute rock bottom.

I sighed.

"Doc..." I stammered, "I'm not suicidal or anything."

"I think you may be avoiding my question a little bit."

"No Doc... I'm not going to hurt myself." I insisted, and before she could ask, I added "Or anybody else, for that matter!"

"Hmm..." she attempted to make eye contact, which I

continually avoided "What exactly are you feeling right at this very moment?"

"Pretty pathetic, Doc..."

"You're avoiding your true feelings."

"Guilty."

"I know."

"No, Doc... I just feel terribly guilty."

"Why guilty?"

"I feel like I'm letting everybody down." I began to cry again, "I feel like a failure."

"Craig..."

"I hate that you had to make a special trip down to the office, just because I'm being a head-case and I'm having trouble getting through the day."

"Craig! Would you just stop that!" she relented, "I'm here to help you!"

I looked down.

"Trapped, Doc." I continued to cry, "I just feel trapped."

"Trapped." she knowingly nodded, "And, you'd just really like to be 'un trapped', correct?"

straitjacket vacation

"Well, yeah..."

"Hmm... by, any means necessary?" she led me.

"Yeah." I caught myself, "I mean, no!"

"Okay." she settled her head into her left hand, which was leaning on her desk, "So. You're feeling trapped, and you're looking for any way out?"

I looked down.

"Craig?"

I kept my focus squarely on my feet and the surrounding tile floor.

"I..."

"You need to tell me..." she interrogated.

"Um..."

"Craig..."

"Yeah... I guess so, Doc." I exhaled.

"Okay. Then we now have two options."

I folded my arms on her desk, and put my head down.

"Craig. Are you listening?"

Keeping my head down, I gave my counselor a "thumbs-up".

Stifling a small laugh, she continued "We can either go to the local hospital to have you evaluated by a crisis counselor."

"I thought you were a crisis counselor?" I interrupted, lifting my head.

"These counselors are better trained to deal with those under extreme duress."

"What's the second option?"

"We can go to the local crisis center."

"What's the difference?"

"Well... the Hospital will be cleaner. Have less psychotic criminals at it. And be covered by your insurance."

"Can I go with option number three?"

"Which is?"

"I just leave here and go home... hoping this all may pass?"

"Craig!" she became annoyed, "Read my lips... No Chance."

I shook my head, disappointed.

straitjacket vacation

"I can't in good conscience, let you leave this office without knowing you're going somewhere where you will be safe."

"I'll be okay, Doc." I pleaded, "I just need to adjust... maybe sell the house... maybe find roommates..." I began to hyper ventilate.

"Okay, Craig." she was going through her pocketbook, "We're off to the hospital."

I simply sat there, and watched her stand up, and toss her pocketbook over her shoulder. She was seemingly moving in fast motion, which was an odd sight for a woman of her age. Her desk began to sway, almost like a gentle wave. Gentle enough for me to question whether or not I was seeing things, but strong enough to make me nauseous.

I tried to stand, but couldn't. I continued to cry.

"Craig?" she sat back down, "You just let me know when you're ready to go, and I'll take you."

Fighting back more tears, "I'll be okay, Doc." I sniffled, "I promise, I'll go to the hospital... I just need a minute."

She smiled, "I know you're going, because I'm taking you." She rustled my hair, "You're in no condition to drive."

"And you don't think I'll actually go?"

"Bingo!"

I laughed, and began to stand up. We headed out of her office and to her car.

The hospital was a good five miles away from her office, and there were no expressways to expedite the trip. We sat in some more of the ever present in town construction traffic. Along the way, she tried to make a bit of small talk. I don't recall about what or being terribly responsive.

Upon arrival, we rushed into the Behavioral Health Crisis Center. We were advised to report to the Emergency Room. My counselor pleaded with the woman behind the desk to see that I would receive a quick evaluation to no avail. With that, we were off to the Emergency Room on the other side of the complex.

The Emergency Room featured a plethora of sights, sounds and smells that were anything but familiar to me. Sick people. Really sick people. People on intravenous feeding bags. Everything suddenly went into fast motion again.

I felt bear-paw like hands on my shoulders, as I was guided to a heavily padded chair. A thermometer was crammed into my ear, and a cuff was wrapped tightly around my bicep. I felt as though I was going to pass out. I looked to my wrist, to find I was now "tagged". Only then, I realized the severity of my current situation.

I was yanked out of the chair by the same paws, and shoved away. My counselor guided me over to the waiting

straitjacket vacation

area, "We're probably going to be here awhile, Craig."

I collected my scruples, and excused myself to the outdoor waiting area. I needed to make a few phone calls.

"Don't try to make a run for it!" my counselor joked as I smiled and waved, walking backwards out the automatic doors.

I leaned against the wall, and took note of the half dozen nurses smoking their cigarettes, and complaining about all the bull shit and "politics" that goes on in this hospital.

I audibly sighed, and worked my way through my cell phone to touch base with family.

First, Danielle.

I dial up Danielle, and am subjected to her annoying "ring back tone" until she answers.

"Craig?"

"Yeah, hey, babe... I'm uh..." I cautiously stammered, not knowing my current standing with her.

"What's going on? Why are you calling?"

"Babe, I'm calling from the hospital..."

"What are you doing at the hospital?"

"The Doc wanted me to come in for an evaluation."

"Are you kidding me???"

"Yeah..." I bit my lip, "I mean, no... no, I'm not kidding."

"Are you sure you need to be there?" she incredulously asked.

"The Doc said--"

She cut me off, "How much is this going to cost me?"

"What?"

"Hospitals are expensive, Craig." she condescendingly said, "This little visit of yours could wind up costing me like ten thousand dollars!"

"I've got insurance..." I replied, stunned and visibly rocked by what I'd just heard.

"Craig... you better not be screwing around." she demanded, "You better not be wasting my money here."

With that, she hung up.

I stood there, looking and feeling as though I'd just been hit by a truck. My counselor approached.

"Have you talked to your mother yet?"

"Uhh, no Doc... was just getting to that." I snapped back into reality, "I'll be right back inside."

straitjacket vacation

I called my mother, and advised her of my current situation. She assured me she would be at the hospital just as soon as she could. I felt embarrassed, as here I was pushing thirty with a bulldozer... and had to call my "mommy" to come help me at the hospital.

Before reentering the building, I stood back, and surveyed the environment. I tried to take in all the sights and smells, as I was unaware of the next time I'd be allowed outside. I'd heard so many stories of people who are admitted into the hospital. They feel like prisoners, kept hidden away from the world outside. I looked down, scratched my head, and headed back inside.

I sat back down next to my counselor, and took note of what I assumed to be a cancer patient sitting in a wheelchair almost immediately before me. She had a nurse, and a man who I figured was her husband. She wore a little bonnet covering her bare head, and a dust mask, that was smeared with the blood she'd been coughing up.

I felt such sadness looking at her, and once more felt ashamed. What was I doing in the same place as this woman? This woman, who actually NEEDS help, may actually get pushed aside by some petulant man-child who can't adjust to being dumped and moving into a new house.

In the two hours I sat in that waiting room, I saw a dozen people see doctors before her. It just didn't feel right. The only consolation was that I was not one of those dozen. She did get the opportunity to see a doctor before I did.

At the end of my wait, I was herded into a tiny hallway, where we actually had to stand shoulder to shoulder to fit. I stood there for another half hour.

Finally, I was directed into an examination room... where I sat for another hour.

There was a knock at the door. I excitedly expected to see a crisis counselor, so I could get this experience over with. Instead, I was greeted by a tiny Asian woman, who carried a bright green tray, which resembled a fishing tackle box insert.

"Ees blood work time!" she happily exclaimed.

What???

Blood work???

I'm here for therapy!!!

I hadn't had a needle in my arm since I was a child receiving booster shots. I began to squirrel my way out the door.

"No need to be scare, Meester Weiner!" she sang, "Dees will no hurt a beet!"

Backed into a corner, I lost my balance. I luckily landed on a stool, where, apparently I was supposed to have been seated all along.

The little woman noted, as she wrapped my arm with a rubber band, that I had "good veins". I sheepishly thanked

straitjacket vacation

her, without even realizing that it may not have been a compliment.

She giggled, and inserted the needle. I had to admit, it didn't hurt nearly as much as I'd thought.

* * * * *

"Weiner?" my thoughts are interrupted by strange and unfamiliar voices from the outside. "Man that must have been a tough upbringing!"

Regaining my composure, I realize I'm still waiting for my wheelchair escort. Realizing that I must have been waiting for several hours, panic begins to overwhelm me.

The voices I was hearing from outside were now clearly those of the nurses at the station, "Man, I'd just hate to have to go through life with a name like Weiner."

"Naw, that ain't too bad of a name. I heard of worse."

"Like what?"

"Um, I dunno... Semen, maybe?"

"Haw Haw Haw Haw"

Suddenly, something inside me just snapped. I jump to my feet, and march over to the nurse's station.

Slamming my fists on their plexi-glass divider, I begin to rant, "If we're quite done talking about how

fucking awful my fucking last name is, can someone please take me to my fucking room!"

The nurses, clearly taken aback, look at each other, wide-eyed.

"Young man?" the black male nurse asks, "You is still here?"

Shoving the files off of his desk, I exclaim "No fucking shit!"

Oh, boy... I think to myself, now I'm starting to look and sound like I belong here. The female nurse quietly excuses herself and slowly backs away from the station.

"Ah... Ah... Ah'll call up to the Unit." the male stammered and stuttered, "You have my sincerest apologies, young man."

Looking back and forth, seeing that I now appeared to be the only patient left in "holding", I ask, "How in the fuck did this happen?"

"Like I said, young man... I'm sorry." the nurse whistled through his gapped teeth, "Don't you worry any, now, boy. Your chariot is on its way!"

I return to where I was sitting earlier, the child-size stool. I wheel myself into the nurse's station.

"Uh-uh, you cain't come back here, young man." He begins wheeling his own chair towards me.

straitjacket vacation

"Tell ya what; you're going to have to physically remove me then." I challenge, "If I leave your sight, you're bound to forget about me again."

He sighed, and returned to his game of computer solitaire, "So, son. Do you follow sports?"

"Ehh, a little."

"Who you like in the World Series?"

"I'm pulling for the Mets, but it'll probably be the fucking Red Sox."

"Ha ha, I sure hope so, young man."

Suddenly, the nurse became alert. Looking past me, he deftly alt-tabbed his current solitaire game off his monitor, "Ooh, boy. Your escort... he has arrived!"

I look over my shoulder to see a small Hispanic man, who appeared to be eight months pregnant. He wore a thin mustache that was groomed to the point of ridiculousness.

I begin to stand up only to notice there's no wheelchair.

The nurse angrily stands up, places his hands on his hips, and bends forward ever so slightly, "Where is this boy's wheelchair?" He retains this bird-like stance for a few seconds. I am unsure whether or not to laugh. I decide not to, as I'm also quite perturbed at this man's lack of wheelchair.

"Ehh?" the man mutters, the most ignorant utterance I'd heard all day, "No body says no-teeng 'bout any veelchair?"

"Fuck this!" I turn to the nurse, "Get me a phone, I'm leaving!"

The nurse places his hands on my shoulders, and roughly begins to massage. "Shh, shh, shh." he tries to calm me down.

I turn my head, and look him in the eyes, one eyebrow raised, "Say what?"

"Everything will be okay." he sang, "Julio here will go back to The Unit and fetch you your wheelchair."

I pull my shoulders from out of his grip, "So, he's going where I'm going to wind up, just to get me a wheelchair?"

"Yes, Sir!"

"Fuck that! I'll walk to The Unit with him!"

"I'm sorry, young man... but you can't... I just can't let ya do that..."

"Stop me!" I begin to walk backwards, arms spread, fully challenging this 300 pound man to pounce on top of me and wrap me up in a straightjacket. I point down the hallway, "Take me to The Unit, Julio!"

straitjacket vacation

"Its hospital policy!" the nurse begged, "You can't go without a wheelchair!"

I point directly at him, "Go fuck yourself!"

"Young man!" he pleaded, "I need you to fill out a waiver... a release form, if you refuse a wheelchair escort..."

"Fuck your forms, too!"

I turn to proceed, only to find Julio now blocking my path. Clearly annoyed, he suggests I go back and wait for him to return with a wheelchair. Suddenly, he speaks perfect English.

"Dude, you can either walk with me to The Unit." I looked him dead in the eyes, "Or get the fuck out of my way, and let me find it myself."

Throwing up his hands, Julio yells out something in Spanish. He grabs my bags and begins to walk away. I assume he's heading to The Unit, so I follow him.

As we approach The Unit, Julio takes notice of the ring on my finger.

"Married?"

"Not exactly..."

"You should think about leaving that ring in your locker at the nurse's station. It may get stolen..."

"Any mother-fucker that wants to steal this ring, is going to have to bite my finger off to get it."

"Okay, Sir." Julio sighed, "Just a friendly warning."

Every step I take in the direction of The Unit brings the foul odor of mothballs and bleach. I notice the walls are no longer faux marble with golden mottle strewn and be speckled throughout. Instead, they are carpeted from about waist height to the floor, and are brightly colored squares from waist height to the ceiling.

At least, I'm sure at one point they were brightly colored. Now they were dull and dingy, almost reminiscent of an elementary school in desperate need of renovation... or demolition.

The ceiling itself, was no longer solid. It was now in panels made from what appeared to be a crumbly pock-marked sheet rock.

The smell grew stronger.

Increasingly embarrassed, I look down. I notice I'm holding my left hand with my right, as if I were being "frog-marched" into police custody. Looking past my hands, I see the carpet.

Where several feet back there was a slick white laminate floor, there was now a carpet. A ratty disgusting old gray carpet that looked like a million multi-colored crayons were mashed and stomped into it years ago.

I feel my stomach turn as it becomes clearer and

straitjacket vacation

clearer that the bleach smell was simply a cover. The odor of human shit becomes more apparent... to the point where it's nearly unbearable.

I turn to Julio, "Do they ever clean this place?"

"Yeah... usually last though." he shrugs, "Behavioral Health isn't the hospital's top priority when it comes to sterility. Why?"

"Don't you smell that?"

"Smell what?"

chapter two
room with a view

"Okay, partner. Here we are… the Behavioral Health Unit." Julio hands me my bags, "Your nurse is Sandy. Best of luck to ya."

Hmm... Sandy, I think. That could be fun.

"Thanks Julio."

I stood at the Behavioral Health counter trying to be as invisible as possible. Finally, a thin man with a goatee approaches from the other side. "Mister Weiner, I presume?"

"How ya doin?"

straitjacket vacation

"Ha-Ha, How *you* doin'?" he attempts his best New York accent.

I unsuccessfully attempt to crack a smile, "I'm looking for Sandy."

"Dude, you're lookin' at him!"

Shit.

"Oh, Okay... uh, here are my bags."

He reaches past my bags and grabs my wrist, looking at my bracelet, "Just gotta make sure you are who you say you are." he laughed.

"Okay, you're in fact Craig Matthew Weiner. I guess we'll have to take you in." he snickered, as he took my bags.

He buzzes the solid steel door that separates the counter area from the actual Unit. I take one final look at the outside world, peering down the hallway I'd just trekked with Julio, take a deep breath, look down and walk on in.

I walked past the inside counter, as Sandy was placing my belongings into a locker. "Hey, buddy?" he asked, "How 'bout I take that ring for ya? Ya wouldn't wanna lose it, or anything."

"No thanks."

room with a view

He scratches his head, "Oh yeah... I've gotta get your vitals! Please have a seat over by the blood pressure machine."

As I walked across the small foyer to the machine, I'm stopped by a rather tall man, sporting a scraggly beard and absolutely filthy clothes.

"I need you to halt, right there." he demanded, in an oddly gentle voice. "I must inquire, do you believe in a Heaven and a Hell?"

"What? Dude, I guess so."

"I require you to stop right there." he repeated holding up his index finger, "If Hell were to appear on a man-made map, superficially speaking, of course, what shape in and of itself would it take."

I raised an eyebrow.

"Of course, that is fully and completely taking into account." he continued, "That the stereotypical Heaven were to be portrayed as an almost..." he stopped, clenching his teeth, and holding his thumb and forefinger together, "polar opposite of that of your vision of the stereotypical Hell."

"Dude." I nonchalantly looked up into his eyes, "Good night."

I walked down the hallway attached to the foyer, "Sandy... you can get my vitals in the morning, just tell me what room I'm in."

straitjacket vacation

I hear the rattling of small wheels, and turn to find Sandy jogging after me with the blood pressure unit. "Craig! It'll just be a moment!" he cried out.

I stop and wait for Sandy to catch up. Nearly out of breath, Sandy bends slightly over. "Sorry about that." he exhales, "That was Alex. Least that's what he said his name was... but believe me, he's totally harmless."

"He's annoying."

"I agree." he whispered, "Let's take care of your vitals, and maybe give you a little something to help you sleep... it must have been a hellish day."

"You have no idea, Sandy." I lean against the wall, and allow him to wrap the blood pressure cuff around my arm.

"Everything will be okay here." he reassured me.

"Dude, just stop." I held up my free hand, "I'm getting tired of all the assurance I've been getting today. It's beginning to make me suspicious."

"Ha ha." Sandy nervously laughs, "Duly noted."

After completing my blood pressure test, he guided me to my room.

"Can I have my clothes?" I ask.

"I will have to go through them first."

"They already did that!"

"I have to do it again, its policy."

"I need to use the phone."

"You're not leaving..."

"I know." I sigh and shake my head, "I need to call in sick to work."

"Work?" he tilts his head.

"Yeah, believe it or not, I actually hold a job."

"I'm so sorry, Craig... you're not typical of a lot of the people I deal with in here." Sandy backs off, "I'll turn the phones on."

"Tell ya what..." I bargain, "I'll make my calls, and you go through my stuff. This way, I'll have all my belongings before long."

Sandy's face crunches up as though he'd just bitten into a lemon, he's clearly annoyed, and I'm clearly one of the more assertive patients he'd dealt with in quite some time... at least, assertive, and relatively sane, he relents "Okay, man. You got it."

Before heading back down the hallway to the foyer, I peek into my room.

There are two beds, mine is the one closest to the

door. The far bed is inhabited by a loudly snoring small naked black man.

I shake my head and sigh, and head back to the front.

Along the way, Alex again approaches. He looks me up and down, as though he'd never seen me before. He pulls me aside, the smell is atrocious, and he whispers in my ear, "I assassinated President John Fitzgerald Kennedy."

I knowingly nod, to simply avoid confrontation. He begins to look at me as though *I'm* crazy.

"You knew?"

"Dude..." I sigh, and look him in the eyes, "Everybody knew."

Wide-eyed, Alex begins to freak out. He runs to his room, which unfortunately is the one closest to the foyer. I can hear him struggling with the door handle, jiggling it in a futile attempt to lock the non lockable door.

I roll my eyes, and stifle a small snicker.

As I venture even closer to the phones, I can hear one of the squeakiest voices I've ever heard. A voice that almost sounded like it was speaking backwards, kind of like the dwarf from "Twin Peaks".

I turn the corner into the telephone area of the foyer, only to find an incredibly tiny girl who appeared to be no older than fifteen, talking into a Fisher-Price toy phone with most of its stickers torn off. The phone's

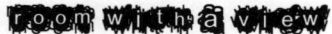

receiver was far too big for her tiny face. She wore thick brown-rimmed glasses that looked at least twenty years out of style. She kept her nose crinkled, as that was the only way her heavy glasses would remain almost in place.

She looks up at me as I approach, and I expect to receive a greeting. Instead, as soon as our eyes meet, she skittishly squirms in her chair, nudges her glasses back up her face, and jumps right back in to her "conversation".

I take the seat next to her, and wait for the *real* phone to be turned on.

"Go ahead!" Sandy yells over, as I see him pilfer through my pants pockets.

I first dial up work. It being about four o'clock in the morning, I get the voice mail.

"Uhh, hey guys. This is Craig." I stammer, "I'm, uh... calling from the hospital. I, uh, won't be in today." I paused, "Err, tomorrow... whenever the hell the next time we work is. I'm sorry... I'll try to keep in touch."

I hang up, not before noting just how flimsy the phone receiver is. It gave an echo when I talked into it. I wasn't sure if anything I had said could actually be heard.

"All good?" Sandy asked.

Motioning with my index finger, I reply, "Just one more."

67

straitjacket vacation

He gives me the thumbs-up, as I stare at the phone.

I feel an odd obligation to call Danielle. I'm really unsure how this conversation will go, or even if we're still a couple. I pick up the phone and slowly dial, hesitating especially before punching in the final number.

The special "ring-back" tone that she had for me was now gone, replaced by a basic ring. I begin to panic, thinking she's quickly moving on with her life, until I realize that I'm not currently calling her from *my* phone.

She groggily answers, "Uh, hullo?"

"Babe?"

"What." she states, without any emotion in her voice.

"I'm, uhh, calling from the hospital."

"Okay."

There's nearly a minute long pause.

"When are you going home?"

"Babe, I don't know." I answer, "I'm at least staying over night."

She begins to cry.

"Babe, what's the matter?"

room with a view

"How..." she sniffles.

"Wha--?"

She cuts me off, "How can you do this to me???"

My head physically flings back, as though I'd just been rocked by a heavyweight prize-fighter. Collecting myself, I'm only able to muster up a, "Wha?"

"You're abandoning me!" she shouted. She was so loud that the tiny girl next to me had taken notice.

The tiny girl quickly shakes her head, her thin waist-length light brown ponytail bouncing violently. She yells something into her toy phone, and slams down the receiver. She stands up and hustles past me. It's now suddenly apparent where the "human shit" smell from earlier was coming from.

"Are you there?" Danielle yells.

"Uh, yeah... Sorry." I snap back into reality, "I'm uh, really sorry. I guess."

"What am I supposed to do with you in the fucking nut house?"

"I--"

"I need you!" she interrupted.

"Everything will be okay." I find myself reassuring her, much like all the nurses had done to me earlier this

straitjacket vacation

hellish night.

She composes herself long enough to say good bye and without waiting for me to return the salutation, hangs up on me.

I sit receiver still in hand, in limbo.

Not only between homes, but unsure whether or not I was still in a relationship with Danielle. What scared me worst of all was I was now questioning whether or not I even *wanted* a relationship with Danielle.

Sandy places my clothes down in front of me, "C'mon, big guy. Let's get you into bed."

Like a zombie, I stand up and begin to walk down the hallway. Alex is still fidgeting with his door handle. Clearly shaken by my sudden submissiveness, Sandy puts his hand on my shoulder, gently guiding me along the way to me room.

Entering the room, Sandy asks if I'd like the bars raised on either side of the bed.

I shake my head.

"Okay." he draws down the blankets, "Why don't you try and get comfortable."

I begin to rub my eyes.

"I'll be right back in a minute with your toiletries and a *Restoral*."

"A what?"

"It'll help you to sleep." he assures making an "okay" gesture with his hand, "Calm your nerves, and whatnot."

Sandy leaves, and I plop down on the bed.

"You a honky?" My now-awake roommate asks in a raspy voice.

"Wha?"

"You a fuckin' honky?"

I turn to look in his direction, to see he hasn't even opened his eyes. I face forward again, "Yeah, Dude. I guess I am, why?"

"Heh."

"Is there gonna be a problem?" I turn back to ask.

"Nah, man. Its cool." he laughed, "I'm just glad you ain't another fucking spic. They leave the bathroom a fucking mess!"

I laugh, "How long you been in for?"

"This time?"

Raising an eyebrow, "Uh, yeah... sure, why not?"

straitjacket vacation

"Thirteen days." he proudly answered, "I'm outta here in the morning though."

"Yeah, hopefully I will be too."

"Heh..."

"What?"

"Nothin, bro." he laughed, "You meet Alex, yet?"

"Yeah."

"Mother-Fucker's a trip, huh?"

I laugh.

"I'm Jack, by the way."

"Oh..." I stammer, "Uh, Craig."

"Well, it was nice knowin' ya. I'll be long gone by the time you wake up tomorrow if they're givin' you a Restoral."

"Cool, man." I scratch my head, "Well, good luck."

"Yeah, bro." he rolls over, and opens his eyes, "You use the bathroom for any reason before goin' to sleep, you clean it the fuck up. Hear me?"

"Yeah." I shake my head, "You got it, Jack."

I look over my shoulder, to see Jack, suddenly fast

asleep. Unfortunately, he'd kicked his blankets completely off baring his naked ass in my direction. Sandy returned, with a small dixie cup, and a pill still in it's wrapper.

"Yeah, he ain't too big on wearin' clothes." he remarked, "That's one of the reasons he keeps winding up here."

I take the cup, and pill, "Why hasn't he been arrested?" I whisper.

"He has been." Sandy shrugs, "But, he always winds up back here... they think it's something functional."

"He's a fucking pervert." I whisper, "I'm in here for anxiety, and I'm sharing my room with a fucking exhibitionist pervert?"

"Hey..." throwing up his arms, Sandy ask "What are ya gonna do? I don't make the rules around here. If I did, things would be a lot different."

I pop my pill and drink it down.

"There we go." Sandy takes the empty cup from me, "You'll be out like a light in no time."

As he backs his way out of the room, he asks if I'd rather the door open or closed. I tell him it doesn't matter.

"Oh, by the way." he stops, "Your toiletries are in that brown bag." motioning towards a small bag on the floor next to the bed.

I nod, and thank him.

There's a small bathroom attached to the room, but I decide not to use it. Not so much because of anything Jack may have said. I simply just didn't want to use the bathroom here. It was almost as though, as soon as I did, it would be like I was really here.

The bed is incredibly uncomfortable, and small. I haven't slept on a bed this tiny since I was a small child. I unsuccessfully try to get comfortable, trying to somehow find harmony between the bed sheets and the damn gown I was still wearing.

An hour goes by, and I note the pill hasn't done its job. Daylight begins to poke its irritating face into the large window in the corner of the room. The window leads out to what I can only assume is a tiny "play area" for the crazies.

Just as I'm about to nod off, there's a wrapping on the wall.

"Breff-fest!!!"

A tremendously wide black woman wobbles down the hallway, pounding on the wall every few feet to inform the residents that it was now, in fact breakfast time. The smell of stale pork only confirmed it.

I turn to my right to see Jack's bed now empty and freshly made. I guess I did fall asleep for a few minutes after all.

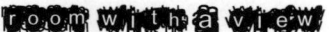

I pick up my bag of clothes and head towards the attached bathroom.

I debate whether or not to use the toilet, and ultimately decide against it. Peering into the mirror, I am greeted by a withered, gaunt version of my face. Normally, I'm quite pale. Now, however, I was a dull gray.

Removing my gown was both liberating and painful. My back had severely stiffened during my "night's rest". Digging around in my bag, I find the pair of slacks I'd worn yesterday, as well as my button-up collared shirt. I decide they're clean enough to wear again, knowing that at least for now, my only alternative is the gown.

Realizing I'd forgotten my toiletries bag, I reenter the room. I'm surprised by a heavy-set younger Hispanic man standing in my doorway. He had horrible acne, and wore a shirt made of the loudest green material I'd ever seen. Hand on his hip, he lisped an introduction, "Hey New Guy, I'm Stephen."

"What's up?" I nod, "I'm Craig."

"Cool man." He bites his lip, "Ya know... we're not allowed in each other's rooms."

"Is that so?" I go to close the door in his face.

He stops me with his foot, "I think breakfast is on." he looked down, "Save ya a seat?"

"That's okay, man." I reply, "All I really need is a

straitjacket vacation

cup of coffee. They *do* have coffee here, don't they?"

"Yeah... it's awful though." his face soured, "Really weak."

"It doesn't matter." I wave him away, "If you'll excuse me."

As Stephen wanders his way to the foyer, I peek out of my door to see people beginning to emerge from each room, herded to their morning feeding. Disgusted, I shake my head, and close my door.

I reenter the tiny bathroom, and empty my little toiletry bag onto the counter top. It contained two bars of soap, that would make hotel soap look tremendously large, some "no more tears" baby shampoo, alcohol-free roll-on deodorant, alcohol-free mouthwash, a tiny tube of baking soda toothpaste, the flimsiest comb I've ever seen, and the absolute most pathetic toothbrush I've ever seen. I look myself in the mirror, and begin to laugh at myself. "Here's another nice mess we've gotten ourselves into."

I decide to wait until after my morning coffee to brush my teeth, and take a shower. I glance over to the shower, and gag. The entire shower "unit" was white, except a yellowish brown streak going down the middle of the floor. The drain was clogged with coarse curly hair.

I choke back a mouthful of vomit, and decide I'll simply apply deodorant and comb my hair for now. Wincing as the lame deodorant "ball" plucks out a half dozen hairs from my under arm each pass, I think of another thing I can ask mom to bring when she visits. I attempt to run the

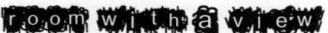

comb through my hair, breaking it. I laugh to myself, as I take note the extremely thin sharp ends of the snapped comb and their potential for self-injury.

All "done-up", I look back into the mirror, and sigh, "Guess it's time for breakfast."

Before leaving the room, I decide to make my bed. For whatever reason, it felt as though making my bed was the only thing I really have any kind of "full" control over, while I'm stuck in here.

Closing my door behind me, I head towards the trough.

About halfway there, I come across a haggardly old man. He wore a "Cher: Believe, Live in Concert" t-shirt that reached to his knees. His bottom lip was so pouted; it looked as though it would bob below his chin when he spoke. His undivided attention had been on one of the many stains on the carpet, until I entered his space.

He looked up, and crinkled his sun-dried forehead. His skin, so red and cracked, looked as though it would flake, crumble or bleed at the slightest movement. His bottom lip quivered, resembling a not-yet-done Jell-O mold. He begins to mutter, "Apple Pie, Apple Pie, Apple Pie, Apple..." he stopped, "Pie."

"That what you had for breakfast?" I inquired.

"No."

He scurries past me, almost annoyed back to his room.

straitjacket vacation

On the outside of the foyer, I notice a bulletin board that I'd somehow neglected the night prior. On it, there was a "guest schedule". I note that there's a time listed on this schedule actually called "Hygiene Time", making me feel about an inch tall. How can I have my family and friends visit me here, and see that I actually have a set-aside "Hygiene Time"?

I took a bit of offense as to the fact that we were referred to as "Guests" instead of "Patients". It was bad enough that we in the Behavioral Health Unit as it is. Now they wouldn't even give us the credibility or respect enough to refer to us as "Patients". It kind of cheapened any of our "conditions", and made it seem like we were just here hanging out, instead of actually "sick". I think about speaking up, but simply shrug it off... realizing, at the moment, I'm more interested in a cup of coffee than starting a revolution.

Heading over to the coffee pot, the wide black woman summoned me, "Weiner!"

I turn, "Craig."

"Did I say something wrong?" she sarcastically retorts, over emphasizing every syllable she says.

"I go by Craig." my eyes narrow, "Call me Craig."

She rolls her eyes, and sarcastically utters, "Issues..."

"You got a problem?"

room with a view

"Nah, I just need your vitals, *Craig*."

"They just *took* my vitals."

"An' now I'm gonna." she grabs my sleeve, "Shit, boy. Just take it easy."

I sit down and again get my temperature and blood pressure taken. I note that her name tag reads "Roshawn."

"Okay, done." she rolls her eyes, "I hope I didn't ruin your day."

"Readings were the same as last night, huh?" I remark.

"Get yo' damn food, boy." she points to a stack of food trays, "you betta watch yo' sharp mouth."

I stand up, and head directly for the coffee pot, "Is this regular or decaf?"

"You pain in the ass!"

"Excuse me?"

"It's regular... it's some weak shit though."

I pour a cup, and note there's no sugar. I again turn to Roshawn, "Sugar?"

"What you call me, boy?"

"Do we have any sugar?"

straitjacket vacation

"Do you *see* any sugar?"

I exhale deeply, and decide that in this case, discretion may be the better part of valor. I make my way to the food trays, and see that they've already been accounted for.

"Roshawn?"

She looks up, as though I'm the bane of her current existence, "Hmmm?"

"My food?"

"Oh, shit, you is new, huh?"

"Yeah."

"Sorry son, looks like you been forgotten." she laughs, "Ah'm just shittin' ya. I'll call down to the kitchen and get you some grub."

I hold up my hand, "That's okay. I'll wait for lunch."

I turn to head into the "day-room" where all the guests were huddled, eating their breakfasts.

"Yo' Welcome!" Roshawn yells.

I wave.

Upon entering the "Day Room", I immediately take

notice of the television set. Children's Programming was on, Sesame Street or something like it. It had puppets, regardless. I'm shocked by the fact that these "guests" are all seemingly transfixed on Elmo or whatever the fuck is on the TV.

I lean against the back wall, and blow on my coffee. I first survey my surroundings, as I'm apt to do. To my left there's a book case full of mildewy looking old board games and puzzles. On top of those, there were some magazines that were at least a decade old. The wall was full of "guest-made" collages and artwork. It made a refrigerator full of a Kindergartners art look like The Sistine Chapel.

To my right, there are some "Twelve Step" program posters and brochures. The brochures instantly grabbed my attention, as they were something I knew I could take back to my room and read, alone and away from all these people. Before investigating my surroundings any more, I grab a handful of brochures and head back towards my room.

I pass by Roshawn at the counter, "We gon' need some more yo' blood, Wei-, err, Craig."

"They *took* my blood yesterday." I spread my arms.

"We need to see how yo' pills is workin'."

"They haven't *given* me any pills yet!"

She rolls her eyes at me, and looks back down into her magazine, "Mm-Hmm."

straitjacket vacation

I head back towards my room, and stop halfway. I turn around and head back to Roshawn, "Hey, any chance someone can clean my bathroom?"

"Ha, you were in there with Jack!"

"Yeah, why?"

She nearly choked on her diet soda, "That boy would yank out his pubic hairs to make his penis look bigger."

I nearly do a spit-take, "Say what?"

"Yeah, boy's got inferiority issues."

"Should you be telling me this?"

"Pshhh..." she rolls her eyes again, "Don't be an asshole."

I turn, and head back to the room. My trek is again interrupted. This time by an older woman, whose left arm was heavily bandaged, "Doctor?" she called out from her bed.

I stop at her doorway.

"Doctor." she continued, "When can I have my pills?"

"I'm sorry, ma'am." I scratched my head, "I'm not the doctor."

"You're kidding me." she sits up, "Just look at how you're dressed."

room with a view

"You can't fool me--" she stops, noticing my bracelet. "What are *you* in for?"

"Anxiety, ma'am." I respectfully nod.

"Don't you wanna know why I'm in here?"

"I wouldn't want to intrude..."

"Nonsense." she begins to scratch at her heavy bandage, "I tried to kill myself last month."

"I'm really sorry to hear that, ma'am." tilting my head a bit, "Has your stay here helped?"

"Well, I'm still alive!" she laughed.

I smiled.

"You have such a kind smile." she noted, "Really genuine."

"Thank You."

"Da'gum handsome too!" she winked.

I looked down, scratched my head and laughed a little bit.'

"Nah, I mean it." she smiled, "You're a handsome son of a gun."

"Thanks ma'am."

straitjacket vacation

"Listen." she stated, matter of fact, "If there's anything you need while you're in here... and I mean ANYthing. Just let ole' Ginny know, okay?"

"Okay, I sure will."

She raised her eyebrows, making her forehead wrinkle, "If you need pain killers, I got 'em."

"Pain killers, eh?"

"Yeah, Oxys, Vicodins, Perks... I got it all."

"I'll keep that in mind." I begin to walk away. I suddenly remember Ginny's original question, and I stop myself, "Hey Ginny?" I ask, "Why did you ask when you could have your pills, if you're so hooked up?"

She laughed, "I'm so hooked up, because I keep asking for them."

"Really?" I ask, raising an eyebrow.

"Yeah, they don't keep track of who's taken what around here. All they care about is that we don't bother them."

Stunned, my jaw slacks.

"I'm serious, young fella..." she points her bony finger in my direction, "If that nigger bitch can sit back behind that counter reading her damn magazines without having to worry about us... she'll give us whatever we want."

I begin to leave again. This time, she stops me, "Hey, kid?"

"Yes, ma'am?"

"I don't think I caught your name."

"Oh, I'm sorry ma'am." I reply, "My name's Craig."

"Be seeing you, Craig." she smiled, "Remember what I said, ya hear?"

"Yes, ma'am."

Finally making my way back to my room, I smooth down my bed and lay above the blankets. By now, I've already drank all of my coffee, but I had plenty to read. It's my hope it will last me through to my release, which I'm sure will be later today after the psychiatrist sees me.

I cannot get comfortable on this damn bed. I stand up and try to use the cranks to give the bed the shape I'm looking for. After nearly a half dozen unsuccessful tries, I give up, and decide to just read while uncomfortable.

Just as I barely get comfortable, I notice Stephen is again in my doorway. He's holding two cups of coffee, and looks to be wearing just as much as he drank.

"Readin'?" he asks.

I glance up at him, and go back to my "Alcoholism and

straitjacket vacation

the Family" brochure.

"Thirsty?" he nods towards the coffee he's holding in his left hand, almost spilling it.

I glance up again, "I'm cool, man. Thanks."

He places the coffee on my nightstand and leans against my wall.

"What are you in for?" he shyly inquires.

"Anxiety... Nerves." I answer, not even looking up from the brochure.

"I drank poison."

That peaked my interest, I looked up at Stephen, "Say what? Poison?"

"Yeah, Rat Poison." almost embarrassed, Stephen admitted, "Family problems kinda got outta hand."

"Family problems, you can't be over eighteen?"

"Nineteen, actually." he looks down, "My father... he doesn't really agree with the way I live my life."

"That's too bad." I put down the brochure, "Parents can be like that, man. No reason to try to off yourself."

"Well, I know that now." Stephen takes a drink from his coffee, "The groups here really helped me. I think I'm a better person now."

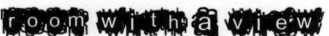

I shrug.

"My father even came to visit me the other day!"

"That's great, man."

"Yeah, I guess." Stephen replied, his eyes now welling up, "Just, now I don't have anywhere to go home to after they release me."

"No way!" I sit up, now paying full attention to his story, "Where are you gonna go?"

"The hospital gave me a sheet with group homes on it." he shrugs, "They'll even pay for my taxi, if I can find one with an empty bed."

I hesitate to say anything, but finally ask, "The hospital's gonna kick out a suicidal kid, who's got no home to go back to?"

"Yeah, man. I don't have insurance." He takes another sip of coffee, "They're saving my bed here for someone that can afford it."

"Well, that's awfully fucked up." I note.

Stephen shrugs, "It is, what it is. I guess." putting down his empty cup, and motioning towards the one he had brought me, "You gonna drink that?"

"Nah, help yourself, man."

straitjacket vacation

"Thanks."

The sound of foot steps coming down the hallway can be heard, "Shit, I better get outta here."

"Yeah, man... hey, good luck if I don't see ya again."

"You aren't going to any of the groups?" he asks.

"Nah, think I'll sit those out." I scrunch my face, and wave him off.

"Okay, man..." he shrugs, "But, I think you ought to at least try one out."

"I'll think about it."

With that Stephen leaves, and I go back to my brochures.

chapter three
group therapy

    The air in the room begins to seemingly coagulate with the foul smell of urine as it's heated by the summer sun. I seem to have picked the perfect day to visit the hospital... the day when the air conditioner goes out. Still lying in bed reading the brochures... seven in total, two in Spanish, I turn to push the "Nurse Call" button only to find there isn't one.

    "Figures." I mutter to myself.

    I stand up, and head towards the door. The urine smell reminds me that I haven't yet used the toilet. At this point, my bladder was so full that I could almost taste it. I decide that, I'd have to try to use the

straitjacket vacation

bathroom at this point.

Standing in front of the toilet, I look down to see another bushel of Jack's pubic hair sitting on the tank. Literally chewing back bile, I take a few shallow breaths and attempt to go.

There's suddenly a knocking on my bathroom door that stops me in my tracks. It appears as though, at this time, I won't actually be able to use the facilities.

I answer the door. I'm greeted by Roshawn.

"Craig?"

"Yeah?"

"Just makin' sure you's still alive!" she laughs, and looks down towards my crotch, "I hope I didn't... ahem... interrupt... anything."

"Interrupt?" my face contorts, "Are you fucking kidding me?"

"Mm-hmm, whateva." she holds up her hand to my face, and waddles out of the room, "It's lunch-time by the way."

"Yeah, thanks." I hold up my index finger, "Oh, by the way, when's the air gonna come back on?"

Stopping dead in her tracks, she turns around with a wicked smile on her face, "Air?"

"Yeah?"

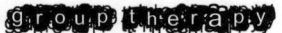

"Heh.", she coughs.

"What the fuck does that mean?"

"Means you oughtta start showin' some respect round here, boy." she points at me.

As I slam the door behind her, I can hear her yelling "Lunchtime!!!" to the other patients. I hold my side, as the need to urinate nearly overtakes me. I can't imagine how hard it's going to be when I have to have a bowel movement.

I stagger back into the bathroom, and realize the inevitable... I had to use the toilet.

Twenty minutes later I emerge from the bathroom, several times nearly vomiting at the sights and smells I had experienced in the filthy lavatory.

I start on my next hallway trek towards the foyer to see if there was a lunch tray with my name on it. Oddly enough, this time, I make the trip uninterrupted. In the foyer, there were no more lunch trays, I motion over to Roshawn.

"Weiner?" she laughed, and pointed over to a quite hefty patient sitting in the corner of the day room, "Ya snooze, ya lose!"

I scowl, but don't say anything. I head over to the phone area, and decide to call into work to ensure they received my message from the night prior.

straitjacket vacation

"Hello, this is Robert. Can I help you?"

"Rob? Dude, its Craig."

"Craig, what the fuck, man? Where are you?"

"Hosp... didn't you get my message?"

"Yeah, but it was muffled to all hell... didn't make any sense."

"Yeah, I wasn't sure that it would."

"So, what's going on, Craig?"

"Shit, man." I scratch my head. "I'll tell ya this much... they took my belt."

"No fuckin' way!" Rob laughed, "You're in the nut house???"

"Behavioral Health Unit." I laughingly correct him, "Behavioral Health Unit."

"Shit, man... that's pretty messed up."

"Yeah, I know. How's work?" I ask.

"Dude, fuck work... work'll still be here when you get out." Robert pauses, "When *are* you getting out?"

"Don't know, Rob. I've gotta see the Doc here before they'll prescribe me anything. Then, I guess they've gotta 'observe' me under the effects of the meds. I should be out by tonight."

"Dude." Rob again pauses, "If they've got to observe you, you'll probably be in there for at least a couple of days."

I wince and laugh, "Dude, don't tell me that."

Robert laughs, "Sorry, dude."

"You wanna--"

Robert interrupts me, "Are you allowed visitors?"

"Shit, man..." I exhale, "Read my mind. I get an hour a day. Six o'clock in the evening."

"Cool, man." Robert notes, "I'll pile the hillbillies into the car after work and we'll visit."

"Ha!" I laugh, "Better be careful man, they'll probably try to--"

Robert interrupts me, "Keep the Creep and the Scum Bag in there."

We both heartily laugh.

"I'll let you get back to work, man."

"Yeah, but I'll see ya tonight."

I hang up the phone, and look over my shoulder.

straitjacket vacation

There are two middle-aged women leaving the day room. One, resembling Bette Midler, was wearing a bathrobe and had rollers in her hair. She was loudly singing some Cher song, which led me to believe she had just seen "Apple Pie's" shirt. The other, was a shorter woman, with shoulder length light brown hair and darker skin. She was speaking with a soft southern twang. She looked to be mildly annoyed with "Bette".

"Bette" immediately takes notice of my presence, and makes a bee-line in my direction yelling "New Guy! New Guy!"

I wave, and stand up with full intentions on heading back to my room. I turn and almost walk directly into a man of about average height, with a gristly goatee and glasses. He stood rigidly straight and was folding the Unit's linens. I attempt to excuse myself and walk around him, and he grabs my arm.

"That's an awfully rude way to be to the ladies." he grunts, "Haven't I raised you to be better than that?"

"Say what?"

"Boy, I know I wasn't the best father, but I am sure I had raised you better."

"I'm sorry, Sir..." I unsuccessfully try to pull myself out of his grip, "I think you have me mistaken for someone else."

"Brian?" he asked.

"No, Sir... I'm Craig."

"Jimmy, let go of the new guy!" the southern woman shouts.

Jimmy looks in my eyes, puzzled. He lets me go, and grunts, "Always took after your fuckin' mother."

The southern woman attends to Jimmy, as "Bette" heads in my direction, "Sorry kid, Jimmy can be like that."

She motions like she wants to give me a hug, "Come on, new guy... we always hug the new ones." I lean in, and she hugs me. She smells like an odd mix of dirty laundry, and shaving cream, "What are you in for?"

"Anxiety."

"Anxiety? Hey!" she leans over to the southern woman, "New guy's in for anxiety, too!"

"What are you talking about?"

"No offense, new guy..." the southern lady twangs, "That's what they all say."

"Okay... what do you *want* me to say?" I shrug.

Bette and the Southern Lady both laugh. Jimmy is back at folding the linens.

"Heh, Craig, is it?" Bette asks, "Before we continue the interrogation." she inhales as though she were taking a drag of a cigarette, "My name is Jean, and this here

straitjacket vacation

Southern cunt is Lucy."

Lucy, elbowing Jean, exclaims "Hey, Bitch!"

"Well, I assure you it was nice meeting you." I halfheartedly salute, "If you'll excuse me."

"What?" Jean laughs, "You got somewhere to be?" she grabs me and begins to dance with me, "Dahling, we got all day and night to dance dance dance!"

"Hey, lady!" I pull away, "Just let me get back to my room."

"Ooh, this one's a prude." Jean laughs. She looks over to Roshawn and mockingly puffs out her lips, "Say, Soul Sista, why is all da cute one's be prudes?"

Roshawn looks up and rolls her eyes. She notices Jimmy folding the linens, "Jimmy, how many God damn time's do I have to tell you to leave the fucking towels be?"

He doesn't even look in her direction. "Jimmy!" She exclaims, "Get back to your damn room!" she stands up, "Now I gotta have all the fucking linens re-washed after your grubby fucking hands touched them!"

Jimmy's face turned a beet-red, he looks up to Roshawn... "Listen!" he pauses, "I'm very very sorry, ma'am. It won't happen again." He bites down on his bottom lip, and heads back to his room.

He glances back to me, "You be a good boy, hear?"

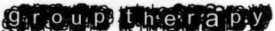

Confused, I nod.

"Now, where were we?" Jean asks, spinning me around.

"I was heading back to my room until visiting hour."

"Oh, don't be like that." Lucy begs, "Just sit a spell." she uncomfortably looks in Jean's direction, "Please?"

I stifle a small laugh and nod.

"Alright! New guy's gonna hang out with us!" Jean sarcastically cheers.

As we were about to enter the day room, I can hear my name being called. I turn to see a rail thin man who was at least a head's length taller than anyone in the Unit. He's wearing a sweater vest even though it's the middle of the summer. He was a full gray beard. He appears to be Indian, but had no trace of an accent. I raise my hand as if to greet him. He looks right past me, and calls Lucy's name too.

Roshawn stands up, and calls the both of us over to the counter. The tall man, without as much as a greeting, turns around, loudly sighs and leaves the Unit.

"That's the medical doctor." Roshawn says, over emphasizing every syllable as though Lucy and I were both mentally retarded. "He's going to see if you're med-i-ca-ll-y ab-le to be treat-ed here."

Lucy jokingly nudges me with her elbow, "Yessum

straitjacket vacation

ma'am, we both be goin' to see da doc-tuh."

I smile.

"I'll buzz you out." Roshawn barks.

The large steel door emits an echoed buzzing, and we're freed to leave the Unit. There were five chairs all lined up down the hallway, that I'd either neglected to notice on my way in, or were newly placed. "Sit." Roshawn demands.

We both sit down. Lucy looks over to me, "Scared?"

I look down, "Nah."

"Liar."

I laugh.

"In a place like this, ya just gotta take everything for what it is." she pauses, "People here are... different."

My head bobs, as I laugh out my nose.

"Don't mind Jean, she's a freak." she stops again, "Also, don't believe a word she says."

I look over, "Yeah, she's a bit off, eh?"

"Yeah." she smirks, "And don't let her get into your room."

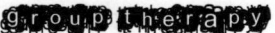

I laugh.

"I mean it, Craig." she intentionally raises an eyebrow, "Don't let her in your room."

"Okay..." I exhale, "Thanks for the tip."

"Jimmy's a great guy... he's just really troubled."

"He's a bit scary."

"He's not gonna hurt you." she shook her head, "He thinks you're his son."

"I kinda figured."

"His son just passed a few weeks ago." she sighed, "All he's got left is a picture of him."

I look up, but before I can say anything, Lucy notes, "You do resemble him quite a bit."

I sigh, "Great..."

"He's harmless, really." she smiled.

She continued, mentioning names that were familiar, and names that were not, but I had kind of phased out. I held up my hand, and asked, "How long have you been here to know so much about the place?"

"Got here yesterday."

"No shit?" I raise an eyebrow.

straitjacket vacation

She laughs, "By the end of today, you'll know everybody's dirty laundry." she pauses, "And they'll know yours."

I begin to shake my head.

"Trust me, Craig." she wags her finger at me, "I was the same as you... the insanity..." she pauses, "they say, is infectious."

We both laugh.

"How about this doctor?" I ask, "Like we're not even good enough to look at."

"This is your first time in Behavioral Health, huh?" she notes.

"Yeah."

"We're human garbage to the hospital." she shrugs, "Nobody wants to admit we're even here."

"Lucy?" the doctor interrupts, staring straight over our heads.

Lucy stands up, and looks down at me, "No worries, Craig." she playfully holds up her fists, "I'll take care of this guy for ya."

I laugh, and she winks.

Lucy spends the better part of a half hour in the

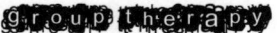

doctor's examination room, leaving me alone to collect my thoughts. My thoughts begin to flow towards Danielle, and the amount of disappointment I have in her... and us.

Several of the things she'd said the past couple of days keep replaying in my head on a loop. I begin to dread the upcoming visitation hour, as I'm unsure as to what it will bring.

Will Danielle show up? Do I want Danielle to show up? What will happen if Danielle shows up? How will I feel if Danielle shows up? How will I feel if she doesn't?

On top of all this, I have co-workers coming to visit. I think about my current surroundings, and fear their arrival. What will they think? After seeing me among these people will I lose their respect? Will I be able to return to work? Will I be as effective at work as I always had been?

I start to calm myself down, when the eight-hundred pound elephant drops on my chest. The house.

My palms are getting sweaty. I begin to dry them on my slacks... leaving dull hand-prints, my breath and heart rate increase. Dizziness enters my head quickly followed by nausea. I feel as though my head and chest are about to explode, when I hear, "Ay yai yai, los locos."

I turn to see a tiny Hispanic woman pulling a custodial trash can towards the Unit.

I stand up in her way, "What did you just say?"

straitjacket vacation

"Nurse?" she looks past me to the counter.

"What. Did. You. Just. Say?"

"Nurse??? Ayudame! Help!"

"Craig, would you sit the fuck down, and let this lady do her job!" Roshawn yells.

I turn, to see her holding a phone, "I'll call Security, Craig." she makes a "tough" face, "Don't you test me, hear?"

I look at the custodian, crack my knuckles, and sit back down.

Lucy walks past, smiling, "Down boy!"

I smile and shake my head.

"Craig..." I hear a droll voice, "Weiner..." by the time I turn around; the doctor had already reentered his examination room.

Upon entering the examination room, I'm greeted by the doctor's back. He's begins talking, without even turning around, "Take a seat."

I hop up on the table as he turns around. Before making eye contact, he buries his eyes into my file. "There's blood in your urine."

"Excuse me?" I say, just trying to get this guy took look at me.

group therapy

"Last night, we took a urine sample. There was blood in it."

"Oh, okay."

"Any allergies?"

"None--" I'm cut off.

"That you know of. Okay." he continues, not skipping a beat, "Any history of family illness?"

"None--" I'm again cut off.

"That you know of. Okay." He turns and begins typing on his computer, "Be sure to check into the blood in your urine."

I nod, and await my dismissal. I sit for about a minute.

"Are you still here?" the doctor sarcastically asks.

"Asshole." I hop off the table, and leave the room.

"Don't be difficult." I hear him drolly say as I head back towards the Unit, using the wall as a guide. Roshawn "buzzes" me back in. As I pass by the counter, I ask when my psychiatrist would be arriving. She laughed, and advised me that I had the "night shrink", and I'd have to wait several more hours before I would even be given a rough estimate on when I may be getting out of here.

103

straitjacket vacation

My head slumps down, defeated. I could almost cry, however, for whatever reason I'm suddenly drained of most of my energy. I audibly sigh, "Okay. Thanks."

I consider going back to my room to sulk, but I get distracted by a bit of uproarious laughter coming from out of the day room.

Curious, I turn around to observe what was going on, only to find Stephen entertaining the room with some silly songs. On the television, there appears to be a showing of open-heart surgery. I lean into the doorway, and begin to watch.

Lucy motions for me to come over and sit down next to her on the couch. I reluctantly oblige... each step closer to the group makes me feel less sane, and even more insecure.

After about five minutes, an older man in a casual looking suit enters and greets the room.

"Hello everyone." he softly states, "My name is Doctor Sean, and I'm here today to... help bridge some gaps we may be coming to, and... hopefully help you all share your feelings." he pauses, and strokes his goatee, "Maybe even understand your feelings."

He continues to speak as he stands before the group. He stood in a very gentlemanly fashion, not looking down on us. It was almost as though he respected all of us, before even meeting us. I instantly trusted him, which is an absolute oddity for me. He looked as though he actually believed in what he was saying, and genuinely wanted to

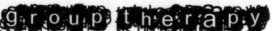

share his knowledge and possibly assist us. His soft voice, almost hypnotic, kept me entranced.

"Group Time!" Roshawn yells, snapping me out of my current delirium.

As I start to stand up to leave the room, Lucy tugs on my sleeve and shakes her head, "Stay... Doctor Sean's real fun."

I sigh, and sit back down.

"I'd like to do something a bit different today." Doctor Sean stated, as he was rearranging all of the chairs in the room into a circular formation, "Today... we're going to sit in, what I like to call, a Sharing Circle."

I would have laughed, had I not seen the face Doctor Sean was making when he said "Sharing Circle". Doctor Sean was apparently a man who didn't take himself too seriously, which put me at ease... and made it less likely that I would say anything to insult him.

Eight of the Unit's "guests" (myself included) remained in the day room for the Sharing Circle Session. The good Doctor sat in the middle. He pointed to Alex, who was directly to my left and asked him to begin.

"I'm Alex." he said, glaring at Doctor Sean incredulously, "I'm going back to my room."

"Oh, come on Alex!" Jean pleaded, "You *always* leave group!"

straitjacket vacation

"I apologize to the floor if my leaving inconveniences you all in any way." Alex states, without any of the venom or sarcasm that I had expected that line to come with.

"You're free to go, Alex." Doctor Sean interjects, throwing up his arm.

As Alex leaves the day room, walking backwards, he stares a hole through Doctor Sean the whole way, "Let us continue."

"Going clockwise." Doctor Sean points to "Apple Pie" who was no longer wearing his Cher shirt.

"I'm Charlie--"

The room, sans me, interrupts with a "Hi, Charlie!"

"Yeah, yeah, yeah..." Charlie sighs, "I'm here because I'm a filthy fucking crack head, and I keep trying to kill myself."

Doctor Sean holds up his hand, "Why would you refer to yourself like that?"

"It's not me man..." Charlie mutters, sarcastically laughing, bottom lip flapping along, "Its fucking society. Society's given up on me."

Sean holds his pen up to his lips, "I don't agree, and I know I haven't given up on you... but, go on."

"Shit, dude." his eyes narrow, "Society's given up on

me, just like it's given up on all of you mother fuckers." he says, as he points around the circle, "Nobody here can count on a fucking thing from anybody."

With nearly a twinkle in his eye, Doctor Sean looks around the circle. His cheeks appear as rosy as Santa Claus'. Finally settling on Charlie, he says "I'd like to think... that if you really believed that... you wouldn't be sitting in this circle now." he pauses, before throwing up both arms in a very histrionic fashion, "None of you would be!"

Charlie scowls, leans back in his chair, and begins to violently scratch his stomach, "Maybe you're right, man." he grunts, "Hell, and maybe not... what the fuck do I know?"

Sighing and looking down to his pad, Sean, with a sarcastic "you win" look on his face shrugs and says, "Fair enough, Charlie... Moving on."

"Hi, I'm Stephen!"

"Hi, Stephen!"

"Hi everybody!" Stephen waves, "I'm here because I attempted suicide." he speaks with an odd rhythmic hiccupping sound. He pauses and looks up at the room's lights, as though he's trying to figure out what to say next, "But... I think I'm all better now thanks to the great support from my new friends!"

An uncomfortable, "Aww..." fills the room and the women all stand up and hug him.

straitjacket vacation

Scratching the back of his head, Doctor Sean asks the ladies to sit down so the group can continue.

Next up is the woman who ate my lunch. As I had previously mentioned, she was quite large. She was oddly wearing a pair of cow-print pajamas. She had long hairs on her chin, and spittle built up in the corners of her mouth when she spoke, "My name is Shirley."

"Hi, Shirley!"

"I'm here because I fell into a major depression." she's already crying, "I just can't seem to deal with life anymore." Jean stands up and goes over to hug her, Doctor Sean holds up his hand to stop her.

"Go on..."

I hand her the box of tissues I just notice is next to me, which gets *me* a glare from Sean.

"Go on..."

"I'm not suicidal." she cries, "I'm just sad, all the time."

"Have the psychiatrists here been able to help you?"

"I'm not sure. I'm on medication, but it's giving me diarrhea." she pauses, eyes widened, "Oh shit... I'm sorry, I'm so embarrassed."

The tiny girl from the phones the night earlier

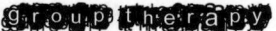

begins to giggle.

"It's okay, we're all adults here." Sean says, holding up both of his hands, "That's what they call a side effect... more often than not, a side effect like that one..." he points down towards Shirley's massive hind quarters, "Is one that goes away after your body adjusts."

Blowing her nose, Shirley says that she hopes he's right.

"Moving on..."

The tiny girl's eyes excitedly widen, to the point where they almost seem to fill her ridiculously oversized glasses. "My name..." she speaks with a thick Russian accent, that didn't look like fit her body, "Ees Victoria."

"Hi, Victoria!"

"And I am here because I miss my family back home, but, what I really vant to know ees... I think it would be nice, eef maybe we can have a pizza party here this veekend???"

The group laughs, as Doctor Sean tries to bring us back on point, "Okay. So, your family... is they back in Russia?"

"No, no... Coney Island." she corrects him quite matter of fact, "But, back to zee pizza party. Do you think you can talk to the office and see if we can have one?"

straitjacket vacation

Doctor Sean removes his glasses, and squeezes the bridge of his nose. The group has now lost itself in the discussion of a potential pizza party. I sit back and watch the chaos. Doctor Sean looks over to me, as though he's looking at the only sane person in the room. I smile and shrug.

"Moving on..."

"My name's Jean... Hi everybody!"

"Hi, Jean!"

She holds up her stitched wrists, and laughs "I'm here because… well, I cried for help!"

This was the first time I'd ever seen freshly slit wrists. My stomach turns a bit, and my face contorts.

"I received an ultimatum from a gentleman I had been seeing, and my husband threatened to take my kids away from me." she's still laughing, "Now, my mother thinks I'll hurt my babies... and they're all joining up to take me to court as soon as I'm let out of here." Now, she's crying, "So, I guess I just needed some 'me' time... so, I slit my fucking wrists." Now she's laughing and crying. It's becoming more and more uncomfortable, as she continues to babble... bringing up substance abuse and pain-killer addictions, male prostitutes, incest, and stealing. All the while, talking about how she has two very young children that she's raising more or less alone.

Lucy rolls her eyes and shakes her head in disgust. Something told me that part of Jean's story either hit a group therapy

little too close to home for her or she simply wasn't buying it.

With a shocked look on his face, all Doctor Sean can mutter is, "Moving on..."

"Hi, mah name's Lucy!"

"Hi, Lucy!"

"I'm here because I'm bi-polar. This is my third visit to Behavioral Health."

"How has this visit served you?" Sean inquires.

"It's too soon to tell." Lucy twangs, "I like it so far, though."

"Great, great... moving on..."

"Hi, I'm Craig."

"Hi, Craig!"

"Yeah, how's it going?" I stammer, "I'm here for severe panic attacks."

"Panic attacks?" Sean ponders, "Hmm..."

"Yeah... I just had a lot of things happen at once." I justify, "My head couldn't take it anymore. Everything turned white"

Doctor Sean smiles, and exhales a small laugh, "I

guess that's one way of describing it. Sometimes your brain can only process so much before shutting itself down."

He goes around the room one more time to see if anyone had anything to add. The only thing that was brought up again was the potential pizza party which wasted the remaining twenty minutes of our "sharing circle". The Doctor dismissed the group, only after he promised to ask the staff if we could have a pizza party.

Everybody leaves the day room, and the custodian is waiting at the door with her vacuum. I stay behind, and thank Doctor Sean for the group. He tells me that I was the first person to ever thank him for doing his job. I shrug and exit the room. As I leave, I glare at the custodian.

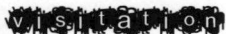

chapter four
visitation

It's nearing dinner time, and the heat in my room is unbearable. My stomach turns with thoughts of world's colliding as I'm soon to be joined by friends, family and my potentially ex-fiancée. I never enjoyed being the center of attention although I sometimes consider myself a performer. An entertainer, who can seemingly "fall into character" at a moments notice to fill whatever part needed to be filled. From hero to villain, in no time flat.

My breathing is again growing rapid. I try to talk myself into feeling better, just by repeating in my head that I'm in the hospital. I realize that I haven't been given any medication yet, and it brings more than a bit of anger into my mix of emotions. I feel like I'm in prison

straitjacket vacation

holding, still waiting for my sentence to be passed down.

Powerlessness overwhelms me. I think its Friday, but I can't be positive. I think I read something on the "guest bulletin board" about there not being any discharges on Sundays. I need to be released tomorrow, as it's becoming more and more apparent that I won't be leaving tonight.

I lay in the bed, looking at the ceiling. Already having read each brochure I'd swiped from the foyer twice, there was nothing left for me to do to entertain myself. I thought about maybe taking a shower before my visitors arrived, however, a quick glance into my bathroom told me that a good portion of Jack still inhabited it.

I return to my bed, and my staring contest with the ceiling.

There's a light scratching at the door. As I sit up, alert, an incredibly frail young boy walks in. He's wearing a hospital gown, and is draped in one of the hospital's blankets. He is shivering, and his eyes are bugging out of his skull like those of an emaciated Chihuahua. He had very weak stubble coming out of his chin. No more than a dozen hairs, all about an inch long. He had a large mole on his left cheek.

"You're not like Alex, are you?" he mutters, and cowers as though he expects me to throw something at him.

"Who's Alex?" I lie and shrug.

"That fucking freak, man." he whimpers, "He was

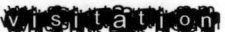

yelling at me for being a Christian."

I shrug, as he shows me one of the many tattoos he has on his body is that of a crucifix.

"He chased me into the bathroom, man." he cries, "I was locked in there for about an hour."

"No shit." I struggle to stifle a laugh.

"Yeah, man." he pauses, "I asked if I could change rooms... if that's cool?"

"Yeah, dude. I'm cool."

"Thanks."

"No problem." I raise an eyebrow, "So, what's your story?"

He furrows his eyebrow, and sits down on the floor, "Just some shit, man."

"Oh, okay."

"You?" he sheepishly asks.

"Anxiety."

"Oh, yeah." he perks up, "Ya know, me too."

"Uh huh." I doubtfully reply.

I watch him as he rocks back and forth on the floor,

straitjacket vacation

clearly not all there. He's licking his lips, and flinching. I immediately realized he was going through withdrawals, from what, I wasn't sure.

"Dude, you alright?"

No response. He's still rocking. He doesn't even notice that I'm talking to him.

The rocking becomes a bit more violent. The blanket falls of off his shoulders, baring his stick-like tattoo adorned arms. The name "Stan" is prominently and repeatedly tattooed on them. His, arms, though emaciated, featured each and every muscle and vein... the skin, almost transparent. His hair, though quite short shook violently as he did.

"Dude?" I begin to get worried.

Still nothing. I think about going to get Roshawn, but ultimately decide not to. I get off the bed and nudge "Stan" with my foot, "Dude?"

Suddenly reentering reality, "Stan" looks up at me. Still shaking, he made a comment about how cold the room was. I asked him when the last time he "chased the dragon" was. He muttered something about "forty-eight hours" but didn't make much sense.

Great. Now I'm sharing a room with a fucking heroin addict. Don't they have rehabilitation centers for people like this? Or prison? It's becoming more and more apparent that the Unit is just for anybody who doesn't "fall" into any of your normal hospital categories.

"Why the fuck aren't you in rehab?" I nudge him again with my foot.

"Dude, I came here voluntarily." he defensively answers.

"That's not what I asked you."

"Dude, I'm here voluntarily!" he states, almost annoyed with me.

Throwing my hands up in the air in both disgust and forfeit, I leave the room.

I start heading down the long hallway towards the foyer. I know dinner should be soon, and I'll be damned if I'm going to be fucked out of my third meal in a row today.

Along the way, I run into Lucy. She holds out her hands to stop me, and asks what's wrong.

"They put a fucking heroin addict in my room!" I exclaim.

"Ohhh." she nods, "You got Alex's old roommate... the kid."

"Yeah, some fuckin' scrawny crack-head!"

"Aww, Craig." her left hand rubs my back, "He's just a little boy."

"Yeah, I know." I begin to relax.

straitjacket vacation

We both headed into the day room. Apparently the Unit is notorious for "misplacing" people's meals; we both decide to camp out to await the trays. While waiting, I tell her the story of what landed me in my current state. I become a bit embarrassed while I'm relating my experiences to her, as it was becoming clearer by the second that I was so much better off then any of my current flock of peers.

When it came time for her to tell her tale, I became so engrossed in every detail of her marriage of eighteen years falling apart. Her finding hickeys on her daughter's neck, and later on finding her husband and daughter fooling around behind the house. Her dependency on pills and her recovery from alcoholism. It really felt like she had absolutely been through the wringer, while I was sitting here pitying myself for owning a house that was too big for me.

It was finally dinner time, and Roshawn was taken off shift. I was glad to see Sandy return to the post. We all line up like the socially inept cattle we are to receive our feed. Tonight's "meal" was a beef stew that resembled and smelled like dog food, a baked potato that was as hard as a rock, and a few stringy woody pieces of asparagus. The smell of the rotten asparagus overtook the room as everybody lifted their lids.

Jean heads over to our table, and we begin to eat. I realize that my new roommate hasn't yet come to dinner, and head back to my room to get him. As I enter the room, I catch him rooting through my toiletries bag.

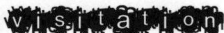

visitation

As he takes notice of my presence, he throws the brown paper bag across the room, "Whoa, fuck man." He's flipping out, "I'm just looking for some deodorant, man. I'm sorry."

"Whatever, dude." I roll my eyes, "Dinner's ready. I've got your seat saved."

He drops his defenses, and his eyes begin to sink back into his head, "Oh, uh, thanks dude."

I turn and leave. He catches up to me in the hallway and continues his earlier apology. I brush him off, and continue to the day room.

The four of us eat our "dinners", and share some stories. "Stan" tells me his name really is Stan. He talks about his heroin addicted girlfriend, who kicked him out of his apartment. He relays how he just lost his job, and was kicked out of culinary arts school. I try to justify my mere presence in the hospital by up-playing my anxiety. Never really touched on anything specific, was far too ashamed to admit, as everyone else seemed to be so much worse off than I was.

Jean's sliced wrists really made it hard to eat. They had a train wreck quality to them, and I just couldn't look away. I know she noticed I was staring, and she didn't try to hide them. I realize I couldn't eat anymore and simply played with the dog food on my plate.

I knew if I ate, I would eventually have to actually sit on the toilet. I feel as though I ate just enough to curb my appetite, without my needing to ever sit on a toilet while I'm here. I excuse myself, and head over to Sandy, who's just finishing up handing out the last of the food trays. It was nice to see that he actually looked at the names on the trays, to ensure everyone got their food.

"Ahhh, Mister Weiner..." he greets me, sarcastically, "I was warned about you."

"I'll bet, man."

"You gave old Roshawn a whole rash of hell today, didn't you?"

"You're damn right I did." I crack my knuckles, "That woman had it in for me from the word go."

"Ahh..." he sarcastically tries to sooth me, "She's actually quite nice. You just need to take it easy."

"Yeah yeah yeah..." I turn to head back to my room. Visiting time was quickly approaching, and I wanted to brush my teeth.

"Have you seen your psychiatrist yet?" Sandy inquired.

I turn around, "Nah... I have the night shrink."

"Ohh!" he nods, "Doctor Singh!"

"I guess." I shrug.

"He's usually here early on Fridays." Sandy scratches his head, "I tell ya what. I'll make sure you're the first

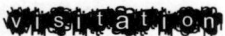

guest he sees."

I thank him, and decide not to take offense to the fact that I was just referred to as a "guest". Brushing my teeth before my entourage arrived was, at this point, far more important than starting a revolution.

I begin on my way back the long hallway, and I'm stopped by the sound of a small ruckus going on from outside the Unit. I stopped, and smiled. I instantly know my family has arrived.

I turn to check out the window to see my mother, my sister and Danielle all turning over their purses to hospital security. They're each given a locker key on a lanyard in exchange. I could note the humor in trading in a bag for something sharp on a string, but I decide against it.

Before they are given the opportunity to enter, they bump into my buddies from work, Robert and Joey. It's a truly strange thing, seeing one's worlds collide in such a way. Awkward handshakes and nods, uncomfortable greetings... and they're going through all of it just to see me.

Several minutes go by before I finally hear the buzzing of the large steel door. I appear to be the Unit's only "guest" becoming excited. It's soon clear why. I'm the only "guest" that has visitors, or is even expecting them by the looks of it. My peers continue about their evening as though there weren't even a visitation hour at all.

straitjacket vacation

Before I know it, my mother grabs me and hugs me, holding me for nearly a minute. Looking over my mother's shoulder, I can't help but notice a small grimace on Danielle's face. Next, my sister, Tina hugs me. While hugging her I shake Robert's and Joey's hands. I finally turn to Danielle, and wink.

"Hey Baby."

She couldn't help but smile, and I know it annoyed her to do it.

"Where do we go?"

"Can we go to your room?"

"I guess we just hang out here."

"Let's grab a table."

I peer into the day room, and notice the back patio area is cleared of all crazies. Like a pied-piper, I lead my visitor posse to the outside with as little interaction from my "peers" as possible. Some hooting and hollering can be heard about how "popular" I appear to be. I kindly smile, and carry on.

Outside, I breathe in the hot August air filling my lungs with its first feast of "non-hospital" air in over twenty-four hours. The nearby construction and heavy traffic noise couldn't even ruin this moment for me.

I take a seat between the two small picnic tables the Unit so graciously provided, and my friends and family

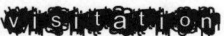

gather around me as though they were expecting me to say something profound, or even prophetic.

Instead, we sit there in silence for a minute or so.

Finally, I turn to Robert and ask him how everything went at work. He gently laughs and tells me not to worry about work. He also notes that the Scum Bag sends his love, even though he couldn't make it that night.

I turn to Joey, and ask how he's doing in his weekly dart league. He begins a long drawn out tale about how his last several dart games had went before Robert smacks him in the back of the head, "Creep! We're here for Craig today!"

I lean back in my chair and broadly smile, still taking in deep breaths of the hot evening air. My mother takes note of that very fact, and asks why I'm currently so happy.

I correct her slightly. I tell her I'm not happy, I'm simply at ease. If I could lean back and close my eyes right now, and just listen to my friends and family converse for the rest of my life, I'd do it. I try to equate my head to a machine that's full of pressure valves. I explain that one of them has just been set off, and it's a nice feeling. The comfort my friends and family were able to bring me this night really made me feel "normal" for the first time all day.

I try to relate some hospital stories, as well as some of the gossip about my current contemporaries, but it appears to be going over everybody's heads. Almost as

straitjacket vacation

though I'm not making any sense, or at least speaking in the right context.

I'm sure it had something to do with the fact that I simply could not stop smiling. It's hard to take a story about sewed up sliced wrists seriously, when the story teller is absolutely giddy while telling it.

My head begins to lose ground to my ever-speedy mouth. It simply couldn't keep up. I just keep talking and talking and talking. Like a balloon that was just popped, everything came out. Incest and Apple Pies, Rat Poison, Heroin Withdrawals, the assassination of John F. Kennedy, pictures of my naked genitals and backside. Talking, talking, and talking.

It quickly gets to the point where I'm actually beginning to annoy myself. Not only annoy myself, but worry myself. What was coming over me? Why couldn't I control it? Why couldn't I stop talking? Is *this* one of the reasons why I'm here?

My mind begins to play narrator to myself for awhile, totally detaching itself to my rapidly moving mouth. All the while, I continue to speak... blah, blah, blah.

I notice Danielle. She's trying not to make too much eye-contact, though I catch her trying to steal a glance or two. Joey's absolutely in another world, examining the bars that encased the patio. Robert was smiling. His sense of humor so closely resembles my own, that I'm sure he actually realizes how funny the stories I'm telling are (at least to me, anyways). My mother and sister just sit, and watch, and unfortunately... listen.

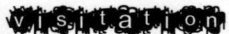

After about fifteen minutes of verbal diarrhea, I stop to take a breath. I can see Stephen approaching the patio door, baring a tray with six small cups on it. I jump up and open the door for him.

"It's hot out here." he comments, "I thought you guys may want some water."

He gives each of us a cup, and heads back inside as we all thank him for his kind act.

"What's *his* name?" my mother asks.

"Stephen."

"Is he Rat Poision, or Apple Pie?"

"Rat Poison."

"He reminds me so much of your Aunt Deb's son, Stephen."

"Yeah, I guess."

My sister jokingly sniffs her cup of water, "Uhh... what's this red stuff floating around in here?"

We all laugh, until we all check our own cups of water and realize she's not joking. In each of the cups there were little "puffs" of red floating and strewn in the water. Like a cloud of blood droplets, there were strings both thick and thin.

straitjacket vacation

As if by design, we all hand over our cups to Joey at the same time.

We share a laugh. Joey furrowing his brow only makes our laugher heartier. He scrunches his face, makes a sound like he's sucking in some air, and begins to drink. We all look at each other, befuddled. Robert finally asks what it tastes like. Joey replies that he doesn't know. Robert asked if it tasted like rat poison or blood. Joey simply shrugged his shoulders.

There are no clocks on the wall here, so I'm unaware of just how much time we'd spent. My mother and sister decide to leave a bit early to give Danielle and I some time to talk alone. Robert and Joey follow suit, only after we let Joey finish telling his dart league story.

I thank everyone for coming to see me, and try not to get too emotional during our good byes.

I turn to Danielle. She takes my hand.

"You're still wearing your ring?" she inquisitively notes.

"Yeah." I look into her eyes, "It still means something to me."

She smiles.

"How can we fix this?" I ask.

She looks down, "I don't know."

"Do you even *want* to?"

"Of course!"

"Okay." I smile, "So, let's just start over new."

She smiles, "I think I'd like that."

"Cool."

Sandy comes outside, knocking on the door as he opens it to inform us that visitation is over for the day. I smile at Danielle and thank her for coming. She stands up, kissing me on the forehead, and walks towards the front, looking back at me twice before finally leaving.

"Also… by the way, Craig?" Sandy mentions with a smile on his face, "Your doctor's here."

I spring to my feet, and reenter the Unit, making a bee-line to the room by the foyer marked "Therapy in Progress".

straitjacket vacation

chapter five
consultation
meditation
confirmation

The elusive and peculiar looking Dr. Singh greets me, and asks me to have a seat while he reads my file. I interrupt to ask what my chances of going home tonight are. He smiles, and tells me to ready myself for at least a few days. My heart sinks. I jokingly mention that the news would do wonders for my depression. He simply smiled, adjusted his glasses, and continued to read over my file.

A few minutes go by. He finally turns to me, and asks what's troubling me. I tell him that it's all in my

consultation meditation confirmation

file.

"Ah, but a file can only tell me so much. I need you to tell Me." he said, with a heavy Indian accent, almost clicking when he spoke.

"Well... I moved into a new house."

He nodded, stopping as his chin neared his chest as though he were giving me the green light to continue. Only I didn't. I was done.

"Is this a *bad* thing?" he clicked.

"Yeah, kinda." I grew uncomfortable in my chair. If something that most people see as a *good* thing was fucking me up so badly, how would I *ever* deal with something that most people would consider *bad*?

"Explain this to me." he demanded.

"Well... Doctor Singh." I stall, "I guess this was the first time in my life that I'm in a position where I actually need somebody."

"You should never *need* anybody."

"Well, I mean... financially as well as emotionally."

"I see."

"Yeah, like, back in my apartment." I say, "I wasn't financially comfortable... or even stable, but I knew when it came to pay my way... I could handle it."

"This isn't so in the new home?"

"Not even close."

"You bought this home with your?"

"Fiancée." I pause, "Well, ex-fiancée, now... I guess."

"You're no longer together?" he asks.

"No, sir. Well, I'm not entirely sure."

"Hmm..." He looks up in a ponderous way, "Okay. Let's move on a bit."

"Okay."

"Now, tell me. Am I the first psychiatrist you have seen?"

"No."

He asks what my past experiences were. I tell him about my old psychiatrist, who I had visited at the request of my counselor when I was going through what I considered a post-holiday depression. An awful woman, who wouldn't listen to anything I said, wouldn't even let me speak. Doctor Singh nods and explains that psychiatrists sometimes "type" their patients before getting to know them. I must admit that this made a lot of sense to me. I'd imagine a seasoned, experienced psychiatrist has to run across several similar "types" of patients. Doctor Singh admits that even he has been guilty of this in the past, and probably would be again in the future.

He asks about my diagnosis. I tell him bi-polar disorder.

"Ahh..." he nods, "Manic-Depressive Illness. Now we are getting somewhere."

He inquires whether or not I had been prescribed any medication, I advise him of my month under the influence of *Lamictal* earlier this year.

"Do you feel it helped you in any way?"

"No. Just made my hand break out in a rash... made me forget a lot too."

"So, you stopped treatment?"

"Yeah..."

"Under doctor's orders?"

"No."

"Hmm... Did you even try to address your concerns to your doctor?"

"Yeah. All she wanted to do was increase my dosage."

He shakes his head, "You are right. She was not listening to you."

straitjacketvacation

I nod.

"Did she at least wean you off the *Lamictal*?"

"No. I kinda did that myself. I used fish oil."

"Fish oil?"

"Yeah... I read about its mood stabilizing qualities on the Internet."

He laughs, and redirects the conversation into a more personal area, "Now. Onto Craig..."

I look down.

"Where do you want to begin?" he asks, removing his glasses.

I look at him, and shrug. He asks, "Childhood?"

I roll my eyes, and the doctor looks at me as though he's just hit the jackpot. He asks me to describe my childhood, and I comply with the best of my ability.

He tries to take me all the way back. Way back to my early childhood. Question after question after question.

"I can't remember what my favorite color was... maybe, blue?"

"Transformers... no, wait. G.I. Joe."

"My mother's side."

consultation meditation confirmation

"Italian food."

I suddenly feel as though I was becoming hypnotized. Each time I closed my eyes, I can picture Doctor Singh blowing into a snake charmer's flute. My neck involuntarily begins to sway from side to side to the non-existent music. I begin to feel my forehead beading up with sweat, which I found incredibly odd, as the temperature in the room was actually quite comfortable.

"Have you ever tried meditation?" he asks.

"No."

"I'd like to try meditation before making any final judgments about your medication prescription." he holds up his hand before I can cut him off, "It may seem a little bit unorthodox, yes. However, in the long run it could be better for you... especially after the *Lamictal* failed you."

I rapidly and loudly begin to tap my fingers on the doctor's desk. He's quick to note my nervousness. I'm quick to note his ability to point out the obvious.

"If you're willing to open your mind..." he snaps, "We can use it to help your problems more than any pill could alone."

"Isn't there just a 'happy pill' you could give me?"

He smiles, and assures me that there is no such pill.

straitjacket vacation

"I could prescribe you anything and everything." he continues, "You will still need to do some real work to start and maintain your recovery."

He returns to my childhood. We talk about my mother and father's divorce. I assure him that that has nothing to do with my current malaise. He politely disagrees, but we continue on regardless. He asks if I was a popular guy at school, and I advise him that I was not. He begins to scribble away on his pad. We talk about my current state of introversion and all around dislike of people at large. Apparently the way I described it was very funny, as the doctor was laughing through most of it.

I tell him I've distanced myself from my family in recent years, and how ashamed I am for it to have to come to me going into the hospital to realize just what I'd had. I continue, telling him about my rocky on again-off again relationship with Danielle.

Out of nowhere he stops me and asks what religion I practice. Taken aback, I answer that I'm a Catholic, though; I don't really go to church.

He furrows his brow a bit, and tells me that he would like for me to meet with the hospital chaplain before bedtime.

I shrug my shoulders, and tell him I'll see him. I ask what my prognosis is, and he again asks if I would try meditation.

I give a sarcastic smirk, and tell him that I would consider trying it, only if we could start immediately.

consultation meditation confirmation

He stands up and turns off the lights in the room. He asks me to put my chair in a reclined position and to close my eyes. Once my eyes were closed, there he was again with the snake charmer's flute, and there I was again, gently swaying, almost massaging myself with the back of the chair.

"Okay, Craig." he whispers, "Picture yourself far away from everything." Every syllable he whispered lingered and almost echoed in the room with gentle clicks.

"Take yourself to a place where you are comfortable."

I picture a place that I try to go to nightly. I've always had problems going to sleep at night, so I would have to concoct silly stories to slowly lull me to bed. It's in a Limbo like place, and I'm on a train car. Outside there is a black star-filled sky, and a milky-white sparkling sea. There is no real horizon, so the two bleed and leak into one another. The train is moving. I can hear it, and feel it. It's moving, but there's nowhere to go. Just sea and sky as far as the eye can see.

On the train car with me are several odd characters. There's an aged and withered beauty queen still wearing her sash. A snake-oil salesman in a top hat carrying a comically large briefcase, a dog of indeterminate kind, a tiny cheerleader and a clumsy fellow who was a mix between a knight and a football player. Whether they're there to protect me or amuse me, I'm unsure... they very rarely spoke.

The train gently clops over the non-existent track,

as the doctor once more begins to speak.

"Try to focus on your forehead..."

A few seconds go by, "Relax your forehead."

"Now, let's relax your eyebrows."

I almost physically feel my eyebrows slide off either side of my face.

"Now, your eyes..."

With a couple of thumps and a bounce, my eyeballs hit the back of my throat.

"Your nose... your mouth..."

My nose deflates and it feels as though my chin is wagging.

"Your chin..."

The weight of my now-relaxed chin pulls my mouth agape.

"Neck and throat..."

My head gently rolls down to my shoulder.

"Shoulders..."

My previously crossed arms flop to my side and begin to slowly swing.

consultation meditation confirmation

"Your chest..."

My lungs slowly begin to collapse. I'm suddenly breathing much softer and slower than usual.

"Now, your arms."

As though I'd lit a fuse, all the tension I had in my arms shot down to my hands and fingers.

"Hands... and fingers..."

Just like that, all that tension was gone.

"Stomach."

I begin to slide out of the chair. The doctor places his hand on my chest to help steady me.

"Hips and waist."

I'm jelly in this chair.

"Legs." He pauses, "and finally... feet and toes..."

Here I sit, totally relaxed for the first time I can remember. Part of me wants to fall asleep. Another part of me wants to stay awake long enough to enjoy my current euphoric state.

It becomes a moot point when doctor Singh turns the lights back on.

straitjacket vacation

Groggy and exhausted, I pick up my head. The doctor is writing notes on his pad.

"We are going to start you on 250 mg of *Depakote* and a sleep-aid tonight. Have you ever tried *Allegra*?"

"Uhh, no sir." I reply, yawning, still trying to gather myself.

"Okay, we will use the *Depakote* and some light meditation to work on your anxiety and nerves. The sleep-aid will do the obvious."

I thank him for his time, and for actually talking to me like a human being. He smiles and nods. He dismisses me, and tells me that we will follow up tomorrow.

Upon leaving his office, I run into Lucy, who asks how everything went. I tell her what had happened, and she tells me that Doctor Singh really tries to push his meditation on everyone. I tell her that I think it may have actually helped.

While I was with the doctor, I apparently missed "snack time". Lucy told me she knew where Victoria hid all of her hoarded snacks, if I was interested. I decline the offer, but thank her regardless.

I ask when the chaplain comes to visit. I'm told that he comes by nightly to do a group session, but Alex usually grabs a hold of him and doesn't let him go as soon as he shows up. I roll my eyes and smile. I ask when the pills are handed out. I'm advised that the "candy" gets dispersed around eight-thirty.

consultation meditation confirmation

I peek behind the foyer counter to check the clock. It's about seven-thirty. The chaplain arrives to do his group session. Lucy asks if I want to kill the hour by going to group. I figure it's as good a way as any.

We enter the day room. This group is quite a bit larger than Doctor Sean's. I lean against the wall by the entrance. The hospital chaplain is a rotund red-faced fellow, wearing a button-up white dress shirt and red suspenders. He is yelling and pointing, while he rants like a lunatic. Everyone in the room seems very attentive, especially Alex, who's hand is constantly raised.

The chaplain introduces himself, as he notes my tardy entry to his group, and sarcastically thanks me for finding the time in my busy schedule to attend. His name is Chaplain Dan, and he is here to help spiritually guide us through cognitive therapy. Cognitive therapy is actually something I had previously heard of, and feel makes a lot of sense. It's where you help yourself by thinking positively, and learning from your experiences and actions... though he explains it a touch more radically. He replaces "positive thinking" with "prayer", which I can respect if not follow to the letter. While I'm on the spot, he asks me to introduce myself to the group. I oblige, with a half-hearted wave.

Alex then pipes up, "Clergyman?"

Chaplain Dan's head shrinks into his shoulders; he clearly has a lot of Alex experience. "Yes, Alex? You may speak."

straitjacket vacation

"Clergyman, would you say that faith would look more like a plate of pastries or a bunch of bananas. In the superficial sense of course, superficially speaking thereof if not totally pertaining insomuch as if it were?"

"I..."

"If someone were to ask me, 'would you say that faith would look more like a plate of pastries or a bunch of bananas? In the superficial sense of course, superficially speaking thereof if not totally pertaining insomuch as if it were?' I would most definitely answer in the affirmative."

Alex intends to keep going, though Chaplain Dan is able to keep his mouth at bay, "I-- I-- think I know where he's headed with this one..."

He walks across the room wagging his index finger, "What he's saying is that there is an extreme difference between the superficial and the spiritual." he further goes on to rationalize, "But there are only few that are truly truth-tellers and fact-finders, who are open to actually take in the knowledge of spiritual teachings, the word of the Lord, and cognitive therapy."

Alex, clearly not amused, stands up. "That's not what I mean at all, so called man of the cloth." he approaches the chaplain as though he wants to fight him, "You are most definitely not a messenger from my Lord and Savior!"

He throws the book he had been holding across the room.

consultation meditation confirmation

"Alex!" I yell, fed up with this guy's antics.

A hush falls over the entire room. He looks over at me, with a snarl on his face.

"Calm down, and let the man continue." I try to reason.

"Let this man continue?" he asks, his face is turning red; "You would choose guidance from a blasphemous oaf like this before seeking the truth from me. Hypothetically superficially speaking, if and only if, otherwise known as, be that as it may?"

"Dude..." I shake my head and laugh, "Did you actually just call the chaplain an Oaf?"

The entire room begins to laugh. Alex storms out of the room.

"Now, Craig." the chaplain says, "That wasn't very nice."

"How much more of that dude are we going to have to put up with before someone does something?" I ask, "I don't know about everyone else here, but I'm here for extreme anxiety. I'm roomed with a drug addict, and I've got to deal with violent, potentially dangerous nut-jobs like Alex?"

"Well, I understand these aren't the perfect accommodations..." Dan laughs, "If the world were perfect, there'd be no need for hospitals to begin with."

straitjacket vacation

He dabs a handkerchief on his sweaty forehead, "Ya do understand that, son?"

"Don't condescend to me!" I snap back, "I'm tired of everyone around here talking to the patients like we're either children, or mentally retarded... or both!"

Lucy peers over her shoulder at me, and winces.

I suddenly feel incredibly alone. Fighting the good fight for my fellow patients, when they were all content to just sit back and be talked down to. The next second would play out in my mind for the rest of the evening. Several faces, looking back at me... defeated, emotionally, mentally, even physically. These are people who were content simply making it though the day, much less, actually doing anything productive, with nothing but blank, empty stares. Bodies one could equate to empty tenements that have long since had any inhabitance… save the occasional pest or two.

Realizing anything that I may or may not accomplish here would equate to no more than a one-man revolution, I apologize to Chaplain Dan. I tell him I didn't think it was very nice of him to lead Alex on like he knew what he was talking about. He nods, and I excuse myself from the group.

Sandy is at the counter, being flirted with by Jean.

"We-hell, new guy." Jean laughs and winks, "Quite the little fire-cracker, ain't we?"

I shake my head.

consultation meditation confirmation

"Craig, we both know you're making a lot of good points here." Sandy tries to advise, "But, if you want to get out of here any time soon... you're just going to have to cool down."

"Yeah, I know Sandy... it's just really hard."

"I know it is, man." he looks around to check if anyone else was in earshot, he whispers "There's tons of stuff here, that I think is in place just to make the gues... patients feel about this tall." he holds his fingers an inch apart.

"At least I'm not the only one that sees it."

"No, man. It's just a lot of the patients here..." he pauses, "I don't know... seem to like being spoken to as if they're children."

Jean turns around, "Ooh, spank me daddy!"

Feeling some of the beef-stew dog food revisit the back of my throat, I excuse myself and head back to my room down the long hallway.

Upon return, I see Stan sitting in the corner by the window, rocking violently.

"Shit, dude... again?"

He turns to me, "He-he-hey, Craig, man."

"You okay?"

straitjacket vacation

"Yuh-yuh-yeah, man..." he replies, "You hear when they're gonna give out the pills?"

"Yeah, like a half-hour from now."

"Cool, man."

I notice on my bed that my mother did in fact bring me a care package. Just below my pillow, there were two pairs of neatly folded pajama pants, two polo shirts, my slippers, my "Man of Steel" book, and some more familiar toiletries.

Stan asks me who my visiting entourage was, and I tell him. He tells me that he's not expecting any visitors, and he won't be getting any care packages like the one on my bed. He began to cry, slowing his shaking a little bit.

"Stan?" I shout.

He stops crying long enough to look in my direction. I toss him my second pair of pajama pants. He smiles, "Thank you."

I smile and nod, "I'll see you in the pill line, bro."

I leave the room and head back down the long hallway. About twenty minutes later the "candy" is given out. The drug nurse is a massive pasty faced woman with a short boy's haircut and an awful dirty looking set of scrubs that Omar the tent maker must have had on special. She hands me consultation meditation confirmation

my pills in a tiny cup, and some water. After popping my pills, she grabs me in a way that would be considered a goozle in professional wrestling and makes me open my mouth and stick out my tongue. I do as I'm told; only after she's positive I hadn't "cheeked" my meds, she lets me go. I advise her that she had best not try that again the next time.

I call Danielle to wish her a good night, and get her voice mail. I leave her a message, thanking her for giving us another chance, and telling her how much I'm looking forward to seeing her the next day.

I begin down the long hallway. First room on my left is Alex's. He's pacing the floor, like a professional man dictating a note to a secretary. He doesn't even notice that I'm standing there watching him, though he's looked me in the eyes at least twice.

I turn to my right. Jean's room. She winks at me, I smile and say good night.

I continue on. Next room on the left belongs to Victoria and Ginny. Ginny is sitting on the floor behind a large fake plant in the room. Victoria is not there, I figure she's in the day room with her snack hoard.

To my right is Jimmy's room. He shares it with an old Native American man, who I've only seen one time for a few seconds.

Moving along, the next room on my left was oddly empty, and I couldn't remember if I'd seen anybody in there all day.

straitjacket vacation

Lucy shared the room to the right with Shirley.

Finally at the end of the long hallway, my room was to the left, and Stephen shared the final room to the right with Charlie.

I look all the way back down the hallway towards the foyer, and sigh. Like it or not... This is now my world.

chapter six
the longest night of the longest day

After sleeping for about half the night, I awaken, unable to breathe through my nose. It's not too uncommon for me to wake up with these symptoms. Ever since I'd hit my twenties, I had developed a terrible dust allergy that would enjoy visiting me nightly. This time, however, the blockage was extreme. No amount of attempted snorting or hocking would do anything to help me breathe. I roll over to lie on my left side... nothing. Same when I roll over on my right. I sit up, expecting *that* to help... still nothing.

"Shit."

straitjacket vacation

I rise out of bed, and step into my slippers. I notice Stan hasn't yet gone to bed. Heading into the bathroom to wash my face, I almost trip over Stan's blanket which he'd haphazardly left laying in the middle of our room.

"Shit."

Once in the bathroom, I try to wash my face hoping that maybe a sudden splash of warm water would help clear my nasal passages. My throat was quite sore from sleeping oven-mouthed, breathing in the dry hospital air. I quickly realize that I have to head up to the foyer; I need some sort of sinus medication and something to drink.

There are no clocks on the wall, but if I were to guess, it was probably somewhere around two or three in the morning. I make the long trek down the long hallway, and find Stan arguing with Sandy about some of his medication order.

Sandy notices me in the corner of his eye, "Craigger! What are you doin' up at this hour?"

"Nuddin'." I snort.

"Sound a bit blocked up there, buddy."

"A liddle bid."

"You think it's your medication?"

Shit. I hadn't even thought that this could be a

side-effect of my medication. I think about lying, and hopefully being given my release tomorrow... however, the sound of my mother's voice rings in the back of my mind, "Don't waste this time." I know that if these pills put me in this type of stuffed-up predicament every night I definitely won't take them. I realize I need to tell the truth.

"Maybe id is."

"Okay, let me put in an order for a *Claritin* or something. It'll probably be about forty-five minutes."

"Danks, Sandy." I head over to the water fountain to moisten my parched throat.

Stan follows me over to the fountain and tells me that the hospital is holding out on his pain medication. He was promised Oxycodone, twice a day... and he's only gotten it once. I try to remind him that he's only been here for half the day, and he would probably get the next part of his dosage in the morning. He tells me that I don't understand, and he storms down the long hallway towards our room.

Sandy reemerges from the other side of the counter, and asks me to keep an eye on Stan if I didn't mind. I tell him that Stan's not my responsibility, and that I have issue with the fact that Stan's in The Unit at all. "He's a recovering *drug addict*!" I say, "He should be in rehab, or jail... *not* in a behavioral health ward!"

Sandy nods, he says he understands, though he politely asks me to change my stance on the issue... he

straitjacket vacation

tells me it will really help Stan out in the long run especially when the day-shift comes in, and Stan tries to argue about his medication with *them*. "Craig, I know I'm a soft touch." he continues, "The day shift will eat Stan alive... and he *will* wind up in jail."

I tell him I'd think about it. He thanks me in advance, and tells me he'll bring my decongestant down to my room when it arrives from the pharmacy unit.

I nod and wave and head back down the long hallway.

Arriving back at the room, I hear the shower running in my bathroom. I think nothing of it, and just figure Stan's washing up. I kick off my slippers and climb back into bed. I turn the light above my bed on its dimmest setting, and aim to start reading the book my mother had left for me.

I get a few pages in; when all of a sudden I hear the most awful dry-heaving sound I'd ever heard. It was coming from the bathroom, and was obviously Stan. My first instinct is to check if he's okay, but I decide to sit it out for a bit.

Minutes later, there's more heaving. This time it goes on for a minute straight. Absolute blood-curdling, stomach-turning heaves. I can picture his throat becoming so bloody that *I* can almost taste it. More and more heaving... and then, nothing.

I sit up in the bed, figuring that if he went through another hurl cycle, I would check on him. Sure enough, this time even more violently then before... a terrible vomit-fueled cough, which, from the sounds of it, through him backwards into the wall.

I roll my eyes, just hoping he isn't puking on the shower floor. It's getting to the point where I'll need to use the shower, and I'd hate to have to add "Stan's Vomit" to "Jack's Pubic Hair" on the list of things I need to dodge while bathing.

I decide to get up and knock on the bathroom door. He responds to my knocking with knocking of his own on the bathroom counter.

"Uh, dude... you okay?"

Nothing.

"Dude... knock twice if you're okay."

Knock... Knock.

"Okay, man. Let me know if you need anything."

Knock... Knock.

The smell hanging in the air by the bathroom was quite foul. It was a heavy stink of sick and body odor all warmed over by the hot shower. I took a moment to sniff myself, to make sure the armpit smell wasn't my own. Luckily, in this instance, it was not.

Only about ten minutes have passed since I'd returned to my room. I now have at least a half-hour to go before I get my decongestant. Worst of all, I really didn't feel

all that congested at the moment, but knew if I became nestled into my bed, the blockage would instantly return.

Wandering over towards the window, I kick Stan's blanket out of the way. It lands over by his never-slept-in bed. The window is on Stan's "side" of the room. I felt out of place simply being on his "side" of the room. Almost felt as though I didn't belong. I look over at my bed, from an angle that I hadn't yet seen it. Made it look almost alien, definitely not something that I had been passed out in about an hour earlier.

Peering out the window, I can see the caged patio area about a hundred feet away. There's a large odd looking man in a hospital gown sitting at one of the patio tables staring back at me. Alex is sitting at the other patio table, reading out of what looks like a Bible. It even looks like he's making notes in the margins.

I can't tell if the new odd-looking giant was actually looking at me. I wave, and get no response. I figure he's either so drugged-out that he has no idea where he is, or he's sleeping with his eyes open.

I close the window blinds, and walk back to my bed. Stan is still throwing up at odd intervals.

Realizing that before much longer I would become sick, I decide to head back to the foyer to shoot the shit with Sandy a bit more. As I'm about halfway down the long hallway, I can hear Stan calling out to me in a fevered cry like scream.

Quickly, I turn and run back to the room. I find

the longest night of the longest day

Stan, shirt-less on his knees in the threshold between the bathroom and our room. There's viscous bloody vomit dripping off of his chin, and splattered all over his chest. He's wearing the pajama pants I'd given him, and from the looks of it, has already christened them with his bladder.

I rush in, and kneel beside him. I try to keep his thick brown vomit away from me. At this vantage point, I can see the red streaks strewed throughout. As I try to pick him up, he pulls away.

"I'm okay, Craig."

"What?"

"Just..."

"Yeah?"

"Can I borrow your deodorant?"

"What?"

"Yeah... your deodorant, man."

"Motherfucker, I thought you were dyin' in here!"

He assures me he's okay. I walk over to my nightstand to get my deodorant. As I walk towards him, I can see the remnants of his evening medication swimming in a small puddle of vomit on the bathroom counter.

I shake my head, and chuck the deodorant at his,

straitjacket vacation

narrowly missing.

"You had best clean that fucking shit up Stan!"

He smirks, and sarcastically salutes. "Yes... Sir!"

I leave the room muttering about what a piece of shit I was sharing a room with. Sandy is coming down the hallway with my decongestant.

"Hey, that's no way to talk about Me." he jokes.

Scratching my head, I tell Sandy that it's going to be really tough keeping an eye on young Stan. He assures me that I'm the man for the job. He tells me that a lot of the other patients have mentioned to him that they looked up to me, for speaking up about our treatment. He continues on about how he feels that I might be capable of bringing some change, no matter how minor, to The Unit.

"Didn't you read my file, Sandy?" I ask, "I'm not good at taking compliments."

He laughs, and hands me my pill and a small cup of water, "Well, I hope you're good at taking this decongestant."

"Thanks, Sandy."

He points his finger at me like a gun. Winking, he pulls the trigger, "You got it."

I take the pill, and head back into the room.

the longest night of the longest day

Stan's doing whatever the hell he's doing in the bathroom. I figure I'll stay awake until he meanders out. I sit up in my bed, and begin reading again.

Several minutes later, Stan stumbles out of the bathroom, "Dude, you see the new guy?" he asks, "Big mother-fucker."

"Yeah, I think so... he's on the patio, I think."

"Yeah!" Stan smiles, "Dude looks *fucked up*, man! Probably has some *killer* pain pills!"

"Yeah, I bet." I roll my eyes, as Stan tells me he's going to head out to the patio to "hit-up" the new guy for some of his medication. He lets me know that he'll "take care of" the bathroom mess in the morning. I advise him to be careful, and he laughs.

Stan leaves, and I shut off my light. I intend to sleep through breakfast tomorrow to make up for the sleep I didn't get the night before. Upon lying back down, just as if it were scheduled, I get hit with a ferocious bout of heartburn. I debate whether or not to head up to the foyer, and see if Sandy may have a *Rolaid* or two in his pocket, but decide against it, figuring the "pharmacy unit" would have to get involved, and I'd be waiting *another* hour just to get an antacid.

I manage to finagle my body in such a way where my stomach acid just barely touches the back of my throat. It's almost so feint that it's actually cool. At least that's what I keep telling myself. I laugh at the fact that I'm using cognitive therapy to tell myself that I

straitjacket vacation

don't have heartburn, after about an hour, I'm back to sleep.

    I can remember dreaming. Dreaming of romance, which to me is more than just man-woman relations. Of course, man-woman relations are romantic as well. It's almost just a sense. Almost like taste, but different. I'm dreaming of a rainy afternoon. I'm sitting on the couch at my old apartment, with a blanket and my laptop sitting on my lap. There is some background noise coming from the television, but it's immaterial to the story. I'm typing up my latest script that would be going to press as soon as it's complete. Beside me, there's a loaf of poppy-seed bread, and a tub of butter. I'm tearing off great big hunks of the bread, and dipping it in the butter. In my dream, I almost exclaim "This is it!!!", as if it were the most perfect moment in my life. Romance. Rain. Creation. It's a dream that I've had before, several times, in fact. It's the dream that you can imagine yourself finding the meaning of life at the end of; however, you can just never get to the end. Today was no different.

    "Soldier!"

    What the fuck?

    "Soldier, time to rise and shine!"

    I groggily open my eyes, and roll over. Jimmy is standing in my doorway, standing perfectly straight, hands at his sides.

    "Soldier, are you feeling okay today?"

the longest night of the longest day

"Jimmy... man, what the fuck?"

"That's no way to talk to your father!" he snaps, "Wash up, its meal-time."

"Shit, man..."

"Soldier!"

"Alright, Jimmy... I'm coming."

Jimmy nods, and heads down the long hallway. I can see light coming through where the blinds were bound up on one end. I notice that Stan hadn't returned to bed last night.

I get up, and enter the bathroom. Just as I'd expected, the shower floor is absolutely covered with bloody vomit. I shake my head, and leave. I can't even wash my face, as the counter is also quite coated with various stomach fluids.

I put on my slippers and make my bed. This morning I wear one of the shirts my mother had brought me, and another pair of slacks. I proceed down the long hallway. Upon passing Ginny's room, I hear her calling out for help. I pop my head into her room, "Miss Ginny? Are you okay, ma'am?"

"Craig?" she stutters, "Is that you?"

"Yes, ma'am. Everything okay?"

"You haven't seen the dogs, have you?"

straitjacket vacation

"Dogs? No ma'am."

"Are you sure?"

What the hell is this about? "Um, yeah... no dogs here, ma'am."

"Oh, okay... I thought I saw them running by. Thank you, Craig.", and with that, she got out of bed and walked right past me on her way to the foyer. It was almost as though a switch in her head had been flipped. I stood there for a few moments before moving along.

"Well, here he is!" Roshawn yells, as she notices me entering the foyer area, "Good morning, Mister Craig."

"Morning."

"Can I trouble you for your vitals?" she sarcastically asked.

"Yeah, sure."

As I sit down for my vitals to be checked, Jimmy walks over to me. He rustles my hair with his large nicotine stained hands, and tells me that I'm a good kid. He starts to brag about what a great athlete I was in high school to Roshawn. Surprisingly, she humors him, and congratulates me on my past sports accolades. Rolling my eyes, I thank her.

"See what I mean, such a good kid." Jimmy beams, "Polite... even to a colored lady!"

the longest night of the longest day

Whoa.

Roshawn takes no offense, simply rocking her head back and forth in a sarcastic manner. Jimmy again rustles my hair, and begins to head into the day room, "Soldier, save me your cereal, ya hear?"

I give him thumbs up, and he smiles.

"Roshawn, when the fuck does he get his meds?" I sarcastically ask.

"Shit, boy... you ain't said nothin'."

"How long has he been here?"

"Two weeks." she recalls, "Came in here like a bat out of hell. Trying to shake everything up, kind of like you did. Guess the apple really doesn't fall far from the tree after all!" she begins to laugh.

"Think he'll get out of here soon?"

"Well, I'll tell ya this much, Weiner. He's waiting to have his gall-bladder removed."

"Really, no shit?"

"Yeah, he gets terrible stones. He's in a lot of pain, all the time."

"Man, that's too bad."

straitjacket vacation

"Okay, Craig. Thank you for your cooperation today. You can head to breakfast."

"Thanks."

The smell of the morning is eggs. My stomach turns at the thought of it. Regardless, I pick up my breakfast tray, and head into the day room. Jimmy calls me over to his table. He's sitting with Jean and Lucy. Upon entering, I notice Stan passed out on one of the couches. I nudge him with my foot as I go by.

"Hey, jackass. You got a bathroom to clean."

"Huh?"

"Clean the bathroom, jackass!"

"Oh... fuck."

"Yeah... fuck. Clean it up before I'm done eating."

"Yeah... okay."

As I take my seat, Jimmy quickly snatches up my tiny box of Corn Flakes, and Lucy asks if I'm experiencing "trouble in paradise" noting my exchange with Stan. I explain what had happened the night before, and Jean tells me that Stan probably threw the pill up so he could grind it up and snort it. I tell her it's as good a guess as any, but I didn't care. I simply want a clean bathroom.

The eggs on my tray are coagulated in such a way they almost remind me of the vomit all over my bathroom. Both thick and clumpy in some parts, just water in others. I notice that Stan still hasn't gotten off the couch. I walk over and roll him onto the floor.

"Hey, what the fuck?"

"Bathroom, Stan. Clean the fucking bathroom!"

"Shit, man..." he storms out of the day room.

I instantly feel guilty, and decide to follow him. Either that or I just wanted to be sure he was cleaning up right. As I reenter the foyer, I'm greeted by one of the most bizarre things I'd ever encountered. There was a girl being led into the Unit in a gown, who so resembled Danielle, that I thought I was seeing things. I would have absolutely sworn it was Danielle; however this girl had several facial piercings.

I was just standing there, slack-jawed, still holding the door to the day room open.

"Thank you, Craig!" Ginny said, as she walked past me, mistakenly noting that I was holding the door for her.

"Uh, oh, no problem, ma'am."

So distracted by Ginny's sudden jarring, I missed seeing which direction the Danielle look alike went in. I head down the long hallway to investigate.

Nothing.

Huh, maybe I just imagined it. Okay, where was I?

straitjacket vacation

Oh, yeah. Stan and the bathroom.

I return to my room to find Stan actually cleaning the floor. I sit down on the floor in front of my bed.

"Dude?"

"I'm cleaning it, man. Don't worry."

I nudge our door closed with my foot, "Dude, I don't care what you do in there, as far as your meds."

"I'm not doing anything, Craig. I just got sick."

"Yeah... okay. Like I said, I don't care what you do in there."

He continues to scrub the floor.

"I've got your back, Stan."

He turns and looks at me, puzzled.

"I'll cover for you, as long as you don't fuck me over."

"Why would you do that for me?"

"I don't know, Stan." I say, scratching my head, "I guess, maybe, I just feel like you haven't had too many people in your life you could count on."

"I'm not a charity case, man."

the longest night of the longest day

I look down and laugh, "Well... take it or leave it."

He laughs, "Thanks, Craig."

I get up to leave the room, and look back down at Stan. "That bathroom better shine when you're done."

"It will, man. It will."

Across the hall, Stephen is packing his belongings into one of the clear plastic draw-string bags. I wave to him, and he calls me into his room. He tells me about a great group-home that he found, that dealt primarily with people in his situation. I smile, and wish him the best. He tells me that he'll be gone by lunch. I shake his hand, and decide to head back to the foyer.

I try to sneak past Jimmy's room, however, I get caught.

"Soldier!"

Shit.

"Yeah, Jimmy?"

Jimmy stands up, and heads over to me aggressively. He grabs me by the collar, "I'm going to show you the proper way to make a bed, young man."

"Dude, my bed's already made."

"We'll just see about that."

straitjacket vacation

We march all the way back to my room, to find my already made bed... still made.

"Well, uh, Soldier." Jimmy stammered, "Maybe you did pick up a couple of things from me after all."

He sits down on my bed, and takes off his glasses. He begins to rub his eyes quite vigorously and starts to cry. He asks me if he's ever told me about his father... my alleged grandfather. I tell him he has not. Patting the bed next to him, signaling me to sit down beside him, he begins to tell me the story.

His father was a very proud man, who raised not only Jimmy and his sisters, but four of his cousins as well. Everybody in his small hometown looked at Jimmy's father as a father figure. He was strong, and worked hard and honest each day. Jimmy's mother died while he was a young boy, leaving his father completely alone, raising seven children. After Jimmy, the youngest, moved out, his father began to date. He met a horrible woman, who only wanted him for his supposed wealth. He owned quite a parcel of land that Jimmy at one time was set to inherit.

Jimmy's father passed away about five years ago. His will had been rewritten, and his funeral plot abandoned. Instead, his father was cremated by the horrible woman, and Jimmy never had the opportunity to say goodbye. He tells me that the reason he's so tough on me, is because its how his father raised him, and he's sure it's the way his father would like to see their name continued on.

I sit, in awe of the story that Jimmy just dropped on me. I'm completely speechless, not only for the story's poignancy, but for its non sequitur nature. For the duration of the story, Stan sat in the vomitorium with an incredibly puzzled look on his face.

Jimmy again rustled my hair. The smell of cigarettes on his fingers was strong and awful, especially considering that this was a smoke-free Unit and he'd been here about two weeks.

Politely excusing himself, Jimmy leaves the room and heads down the long hallway.

Stan turns to me, "Dude... is that your father?"

"Seriously, Stan?"

"Shit, dude." He laughs, "Jimmy's fucking crazy!"

"He's troubled. Just like the rest of us."

"Man, I'd have knocked his old ass out if he tried to pretend he was my father."

Standing up from my bed and stretching, I reply, "Well, I guess that's just another difference between you and me, man."

Almost slamming right into Roshawn, I leave the room.

"Mornin' Meds!!!" gets screamed and spat into my face. Momentarily stunned, I see Stan bolt out of the room. Seconds later, I begin to follow. I notice the ersatz Danielle leaving her room, still in her hospital gown. As odd as it may sound, it was rather pleasant

165

straitjacket vacation

seeing a semi-familiar looking face in this abyss of blank stares.

Reaching the foyer, I stand at the back of the line and let everyone else get served before me. The same squat looking nurse is handing out the medication again, and I hope I'm not in for a repeat of the night prior's goozling.

Stan's given his pills and walks past me with a smile. I grab his arm and tell him that I've got next shower, and I'd better not get back to the room and find him trying to vomit up his pain pills. He sticks his tongue out, revealing two whole pills. Winking, he heads back to the room.

Jean is being served her drugs. I notice that today, she's wearing the oversized Cher shirt that Charlie had worn yesterday. She has so many pills it requires a second little cup.

Considering there are about a dozen patients ahead of me, I decide to use one of the nearby phones to call Danielle. I hadn't spoken to her since her visit yesterday evening; it will be nice to hear her voice again.

After a couple of minutes of uncomfortable small talk, Danielle decides to drop a bomb shell on me.

"I'm not coming to visit you today."

"Why not, babe?"

"I kind of told my parents what had happened..."

the longest night of the longest day

"What had happened?"

"Yeah..." she pauses, "With you in the hospital, for, well... you know..."

"What's going on?"

"They would rather I don't see you anymore."

"What??? You're like twenty-five years old! You're gonna let them stop you from seeing me?"

"I know... but, it's probably for the best."

"I really don't follow."

She's silent.

"Do you just not want to be with me anymore?" I ask with quite a bit of trepidation in my voice.

Still silent.

"Is that what this is?"

"I'm so sorry." she cried.

Fighting back tears of my own, I hang up the phone. The acrid odor of old milk and human waste alerts me to Victoria's presence behind me.

"Meester Craig, do you have troubles?" she asks.

"Nah, I'm okay."

straitjacket vacation

"You look sad. You no need to be sad."

"I'll be okay, Victoria."

"Today I not Victoria. Today, I Michelle."

I begin to laugh.

"You happy? I make happy?"

"Yes, Michelle... I'll be okay.", and with that she whizzed away down the long hallway.

The only patient ahead of me is the old giant who I saw on the patio last night. The nurse asks him if he's like to be called Montgomery, or would he rather Monty. He belched, blowing his mustache hairs straight for a moment. He has four little cups full of pills, and a small cup filled with liquid. Being as though, he's still wearing his gown I can see part of his bare back. There is a huge scar running from his hairline, as far down to his mid-back. He keeps sputtering out of his mouth, almost frothing at the sight of his pills. He quickly takes his medication, and heads back towards the patio.

I'm greeted with a sarcastic smile, "If it isn't the most cooperative guest I've seen..."

"Patient." I correct her.

"Excuse me?"

"I'm a patient here. You said guest. Just

correcting you, as I'm sure when I receive the rather sizable bill from my stay here, it will give me the title of Patient... not Guest."

"Whatever."

"Yeah, whatever, right? Just give me my medication."

She begins to laugh, "Maybe I don't have your medication."

Shrugging my shoulders, I begin to walk back to my room, "Okay, maybe you don't."

"Craig!" she stops me, "Get over here and take your pill."

I walk back over and take both the pill and the cup of water. I swallow the pill, and stick out my tongue to prove it's no longer lingering in my mouth.

"Thank you." she sarcastically snips.

"No... thank you." I smile.

straitjacket vacation

chapter seven
change of heart or random acts

With the morning comes "Morning Group", a group I had somehow missed yesterday. Either that, or they simply didn't have it, I'm coming to find that the "Group" schedule around these parts is rather erratic... which is odd, as the groups are supposedly the only point to stick around this place. I decide to put off my already put off shower until after the group. I had great pride in knowing that even two days without a shower, I was still fresher and more clean than most of my current contemporaries.

This group is primarily a "goal setting" one. We all lounge in the day room and talk about our goals. I was about fifth in line to discuss my goals, and all the patients ahead of me really had the same one.

"My name is Charlie, and I'd like to regulate my medication, and work towards recovery."

"My name is Virginia, and I'd like to regulate my medication, and work towards recovery."

"Today... my name... ees, Michelle... and I'd like to regulate my medication, and work towards recovery."

"My name... (sputter), is Mont... gomery... (sputter), and I'd like to regulate my medication, and work towards recovery."

It comes to my turn. I look around, and shrug, "Yeah, uh... my name is Craig, and I'd really like to get around to finishing up the screenplay I've been working on, and see about getting it sold."

The group lead held up his hand to stop me from speaking. He was a huge muscular black man who spoke with the most condescending tone I'd ever heard in my life, "Whoa whoa whoa, there Craig. How about setting some goals in regards to your treatment here at the Unit?"

"Fuck that shit, man. My treatment here at the Unit is in your guy's hands."

"Well, Craig." he hums, "That may not be en-ti-ir-ly true. A lot of it is in your hands."

"Listen, I'm going to get out of here sooner or

straitjacket vacation

later. That much is a fact. We're talking about goals here." I point over to the heavy steel door, "Do our goals end once we walk out that door? Or do they just not matter anymore then?"

"Craig..." Lucy sings.

"No Lucy, this is stupid." I point to Charlie, "Do you feel any better about yourself because you set the same goal you must have set every morning since you got here?"

"No..." Charlie pipes up, "It's the God-damn fucked up society in this Unit that makes us set these useless goals."

I look over to the group lead, and shrug my shoulders.

"If you're planning on being a disturbance to the group, you're free to go."

"Okay, I guess I'll leave then. I hope I can figure my way back to my room without setting the hospital standard morning goal."

I walk out the door, and see Lucy and Charlie getting up too. I hold the door open for them. Maybe I was actually beginning to get through to these people. Maybe they are realizing that they don't need to be spoken to as though they were retarded in order to get help. I take a second to soak in this small victory, and decide it's finally time to brave the shower.

Back down the long hallway I head, stopping to pick

up some fresh towels off of the linens cart. The towels are rather small, definitely smaller than most bathing towels. They were also quite rough, I imagine they don't use too much in the way of fabric softener in the industrial washer/dryers here at the hospital.

Reentering my room, I see that Stan is currently in the bathroom. I knock on the door and tell him to hurry up. I hear a long snorting sound, followed by a rough cough, "Yeah, I'll be right out, man."

Moments later, he staggers out into the room as though he were dancing with the air surrounding him. He's absolutely giddy, and his eyes are heavily tearing. He's talking about a mile a minute, and it's apparent why. On the counter are the remnants of a line of whatever pill he's currently taking, as well as a coffee stirrer and a rogue puzzle piece from the day room.

"Dude, wipe that fucking counter down..." I demand.

"Yeah-you-got-it-man!" he blurts out and hurriedly rushes back into the bathroom.

"I don't want to see any remnants of that shit left out, man."

"Okay-man-no-problem!"

"I'll cover your ass, but you gotta be smart about this shit!"

"Okay-okay-okay!", and with that, he finished cleaning the bathroom. Now, unfortunately, there was

straitjacket vacation

nothing left for me to do but to take a shower.

    The bathroom was tiny, and looked like something from the set of an old, low-budget science-fiction movie. The walls were beveled, and had odd contoured edges. The shower curtain was nearly transparent, except towards the end where the shower head was. On that end, the curtain had a greenish tint from what I can only hope was mildew. Pushing the curtain over, I'm pleased to find that Stan not only cleaned out the vomit, but also Jack's pubic hair. There were still odd hairs strewn about, but not nearly as concentrated as they had been yesterday. I place my small hotel-sized bar of soap on the little silver counter that was inside the shower, as well as my shampoo and conditioner. The smell in here is brutal; I guess you can take the vomit from that bathroom, but not the smell from the vomit... or something. My stomach grows queasy, and I'm soon alerted to the fact that I'm going to have to sit on the toilet.

    Peering down at the toilet, I must admit that Stan did quite a job cleaning it up. With a scowl on my face, I begin to stack up piles of toilet paper on the toilet seat. I turn the shower on in an attempt to cover up any offensive sounds I may make while taking care of business. Slowly I sit down.

    Seconds later there's a knock at the bathroom door, almost scaring me off the toilet. This is one of the reasons I can't use public toilets.

    "Craig?"

    It's Roshawn. What the fuck is she doing knocking on

change of heart or random acts

my bathroom door?

"What?" I yell out.

No answer.

"What do you need?"

No answer. So I get up, and toss out the pile of toilet paper, pull up my pants and open the door. There's nobody there.

Fuck.

I was finally ready to use the facilities, and now whatever rumbling was going on down in my stomach, has been scared away. Back into the bathroom I go, to try and face the shower.

Climbing into the shower for the first time was quite a feat. The reheated scent of yesterday's vomit was starting to steam up and filled my nose. I chew back some of my own, and decide to try breathing through my mouth for the duration of my delousing. I manage to get myself all soaped up before I had to exit the shower to catch my breath. Standing in front of the steamed up mirror, I can barely see myself. I think back to the last time I had showered on Thursday morning before work, and compare that to this. After dripping all over the floor, I realize I need a quick rinse.

Taking one last deep breath of the "fresher" bathroom air, I step back into the shower. I don't move all that much, trying to allow the weak pressured, lime scale built

straitjacket vacation

up shower head do its job.

Moments later, I shut the water off. Stepping out of the shower, I try to maintain my balance on the slick wet floor. Using four towels, I manage to dry most of my body off to a suitable level. Using one of the towels to wipe the mist off of the mirror, I decide to brush my teeth, and then my hair. Giving myself one last look, I decide it's time to go out and socialize a bit.

Throwing my clothes back on, I leave the room. Looking down the long hallway, I see Stephen sitting on the floor against the wall with his bags next to him. He's either just about to, or had just finishing up crying. His face is red and puffy. I approach him, and slump down next to him.

"What's goin' on, man?"

"The boy's home isn't sending a ride for me." he cried, "I have to find a way there myself."

"That shouldn't be a problem. There's a bus stop right outside."

"I don't have any money."

"Maybe Roshawn will spot you some cash."

"She doesn't like me too much."

I stand up and head over to Roshawn at the counter. I ask her if I could borrow a few bucks to give to Stephen, and assure her that I'd pay her back when I leave. She rolls her eyes and starts to make excuses. I reason with her that Stephen is incredibly scared right now, and he's going to a boy's home instead of his real home.

"You do know he's gay?" Roshawn asks in a hushed whisper.

"Is he really?" I sarcastically retort, "I would've never guessed."

"Why you bein' so helpful to the other guests, Weiner?"

"Patients." I correct her, "And, I'm helping them... because they need it."

She rolls her eyes, and then rolls her chair over to her purse that was sitting on the floor under the far end of the counter. A gaudy forty-five pound black leather bag, with gold things dangling off of it. She reaches in with her two inch fingernails and pulls out a twenty dollar bill.

"I'll pay you back before I go." I assure her.

"Forget it, Weiner." she picks up her magazine, "Keep it."

"Thanks, Roshawn." I smile, "Maybe we ought to work on the same side more often."

She doesn't reply.

I walk back to Stephen with the twenty dollar bill

between my index and middle fingers. He begins to cry and goes to hug me.

I let him.

He thanks me, and swears he'll make it up to me someday. I smile, and tell him not to worry about it. I become overwhelmed with the feeling that I may have just made a bit of a difference in somebody's life. These people around me, these crazy, messed-up people... were just people. People who maybe aren't as well put together as some others, but still people… broken people.

A small act of kindness goes a long way to folks, who don't often get smiled at, or doors held for them, or battles fought for them. I began to think of the bigger picture of why I may be here. Maybe I'm here to help people, or learn to make a difference. Either way, this one moment almost justified the past few miserable days I'd experienced.

Gone were fears of home ownership. Gone was Danielle. Gone was everything that I had been scared of... replaced with hope. Hope in that I could help people. Turn this awful experience around, and make good.

I pick up Stephen's bags for him, and hand them to him. He thanks me again and again. I ask him if he's ready to leave and he nods. I walk with him up to the foyer. Without a word, Roshawn buzzes the door open for him. He runs into the day room, and hugs everyone. We pass each other as he leaves the room. We share a smile and a nod.

I sit down on the couch, and I'm still smiling. Lucy takes notice and walks over my way.

"What's goin' on, Craig?"

"Nothing..." I reply, "You ever hear that saying, 'Everything happens for a reason'?"

"Yeah..."

"There are times where it makes a lot of sense. Don't ya think?"

"Yeah..." she answers, "What are you getting at?"

"I'm not sure." I scratch my head, "I just feel like I've been smacked in the face with a great deal of profundity."

"Profundity?"

"Yeah. It's beginning to feel as though maybe I'm here to help rather then to be helped."

"You're crazy." she laughs, "What are you, the Behavioral Health Unit guardian angel?"

I look down and chuckle. I look back up at Lucy, "Maybe I am."

We both laugh; Jean decides to stagger over, "What's the joke? What are we laughing at?"

"Oh nothin', hon." Lucy says, "Just old Craig here

straitjacket vacation

thinks he's the Messiah, or something."

Jean winks, "The Messiah, huh?"

I clear my throat and stand up, "If you ladies will excuse me."

"No, don't go, Savior!" Lucy jokes.

I turn back, and smile.

I get to the day room door, and notice that Monty was heading my way. I open the door and hold it open for him. He belches a foul "Thank You" in my face, and goes about his business. I turn and give thumbs up to a giggling Jean and Lucy.

Back in the foyer, out of the corner of my eye I can see the little Asian woman who had taken my blood the other day entering the Unit with her blood work tray. She seemed to be immediately alerted to my presence, and hustled over in my direction. Knowing it would be futile to attempt to flee; I just stood there and waited.

"Ah!" she exclaimed, "I'm here to take your blood."

"Yeah, yeah, yeah… of course you are...", and with that I'm dragged into the therapy room, where I give my second vial of blood of my hospital visit.

Woozily, I stand up and continue about my day. I can already see Alex. He's standing in the foyer, seemingly waiting for me. He doesn't say anything; however, he has his beady little eyes dead set on me.

change of heart or random acts

"Ya need something, Alex?" I ask.

No response.

"Alright dude..." I begin to walk past him. As I pass, I can hear him mutter something.

Stopping in my tracks, I turn around and ask him if he had said anything, and if he has any problems he'd like to take care of with me.

No response. I decide to get right in his face, as I despise being ignored almost as much as I despise being condescended to.

"Dude, everyone here seems to be scared of you... and you like that." I continue, "Not me, Alex. I can see through your bull shit, man. I know you're more scared of everyone, than they are of you."

He starts snarling. Bits of spittle begin to build up in the corners of his mouth. His face is bright red.

"Listen, man. These aren't the ideal living conditions for anybody around here." I pause, expecting a response, however, get none, "Let's just try to make the best of it. You stay out of my way, and I'll stay out of yours. Sound cool?"

Burning a hole through me with his eyes, Alex finally speaks, "It is quite the revolting development we have here currently at this moment even as we speak. Therefore under with for the difference between you and I is that thereof the difference between a dozen donuts and a dozen red or perhaps white roses. Superficially speaking, of course."

"Dude." I look down and shake my head, "Start making some fucking sense."

He laughs. An awful, almost sinisterly evil laugh, a laugh without a terrible amount of sanity behind it.

I sigh and walk past him down the long hallway to my room, where I kick off my shoes and hop into bed to get a bit more reading in before lunch time.

chapter eight
follow me

I am only able to get a few moments, and pages of reading done before I notice Lucy standing in my doorway.

"Hey Superman!" she says, "You gotta stop fightin' all the super villains around here; else there'll be nothin' left for us all to complain about!"

I put down my book, and smile, "Well, that's the whole point. Now, isn't it?"

She smiles.

"I'm going to eventually get through to Alex." I say, "I'll make it so he's actually a functioning member of our messed up little community... or family... or whatever the hell we are."

"What about *your* recovery? Shouldn't *that* be your top priority?"

Waving off the notion as though it were so much nonsense, I continue, "Ehhh, my recovery's nothing. My problems are nothing compared to most. I *know* I'll be okay. Everyone else... I'm not so certain."

"So, you're just going to go around playing doctor?"

"Nah, just provide simple acts of kindness that I think a lot of people around here have been denied of, for far too long."

She smiles, "Craig, honey... sweetie... Your hearts in the right place, but I really think you're setting yourself up for a really bad fall here."

"Nah." I sit up, "If nothing else, it'll help pass the time until I'm out of here, ya know?"

She begins to talk again, but I stop her, "Trust me, Lucy. When I'm through staying here, maybe, just maybe... some of the folks here will be a bit better off for having known me... and maybe they'll help someone that needs it someday, because of me."

She sighs, realizing that there's no getting through to me. "Well, Good Shepherd, it's time for group. You comin' to this one?"

"Yeah."

I get out of bed, and we head down the long hallway together. I stop at Alex's door and knock.

"What in the world are you doin' now, Craig?" Lucy asks.

"It's group time." I answer, "Alex is coming to group."

No response from Alex, so I knock again.

Finally Alex emerges, and with him the now familiar smell of dirty laundry and armpit.

I look him in the eye, "Dude. Time for group."

He doesn't say anything.

"Alex." I continue, "It's time for group. Come on."

"You want me at group?" he incredulously asks.

"Yeah, man. Come on out."

Oddly and quite unexpectedly, Alex follows us out and into the day room.

"Ah, some stragglers... Come on in!" the waif thin group lead says. This group is being conducted by a tiny young black woman with very short cropped hair. She introduces herself as Natica, and tells us that she's a Crisis Intervention Facilitator. It appears as though this

straitjacket vacation

group will focus on addictions and interventions.

I simply sit back and listen, as I feel this group doesn't pertain to me or any of my neurosis, though I'll open my mind up enough to understand some of my peers battles with their addictions. This, after all, could make me more helpful.

Natica notices Alex, and looks at him uncomfortably, "What's he doing here?"

"I am allowed to be here, negress." he snaps.

"Okay, Alex, okay... why don't you start us off then?"

"Fine." he begins, "I am Alex."

"Hi Alex!"

"That's adorable, but completely unnecessary." he continues, in his odd monotone, "I was brought here to this hospital by the police. I was arrested three times, fifty-one fifty. Which is to say I appeared to be superficially speaking and was considered to be as it were a danger to myself and or to other people in my immediate and or not so immediate area."

"O-kay, Alex." Natica coughs back a small chuckle, and rolls her eyes, "Do you have any stories about your battles with addiction?"

What a bitch, I think to myself. Here's a guy who's simply trying to be part of the group, and he's being all

but written off by this facilitator bitch.

"I am only addicted to getting high. Not so much in as much as saying I own an addiction to any one pill or leaf or rock or drink in question."

Natica tries to interject; however, Alex would not even stop speaking to even take a breath.

"The police picked me up the other night and they tell me I had six needles sticking out of my arm and other parts of my anatomy. I just meander and pick up needles, so to speak. Being a homeless person such as I am to be currently at this time, I tend to find many discarded items, treasures and trinkets, among them some of the time but not most of the time, are partially or completely used needles."

She tries to stop him again, but he keeps going. She attempts to break into the conversation after Alex completes every syllable. Every word she tries to jut into Alex's monologue is visibly making him angrier and angrier. He begins chewing on his words, just grinding his teeth as he speaks in his terrible monotone. Natica finally hits her boiling point, and demands he leave the group.

Alex instantly stops talking, and looks in my direction. Taken aback, I only nod. He nods back, and leaves the room.

After he left, Natica had some not so nice words to say about him. I held up my hand.

"Hey, uh, Natica, is it?"

straitjacket vacation

"Yes?"

"Would you say that Alex is a guy who's in pretty dire need of help?"

"Oh, absolutely!"

"Then what is kicking him out of group going to do to help him?"

"Oh, don't *you* start... or I'll make you leave for disrupting too."

"Oh, that's not necessary. I'll be leaving in a moment. All I ask is that maybe you put yourself in the patient's shoes at some point in time. Alex is a guy who needs a bit of special attention. That responsibility falls on the hospital staff, does it not?"

"You can leave at any time..."

"Okay... I'll go."

I get up and head for the day room door. With me comes half the group... Charlie, Stan, Lucy, Jean and Ginny. Natica simply shakes her head, and passive aggressively says something under her breath about my not making a point.

Ginny reaches up and puts her hand on my shoulder, "Thank you, Craig. Nobody ever speaks up for us."

"Hey, I'm one of 'us'." I smile, "We gotta take care

of each other."

Roshawn overhears, "Craig, you startin' shit again, boy?"

"Of course I am, ma'am."

Roshawn peeks into the day room and begins rhythmically rocking her head from side to side, "Ooh, you got that skinny little bitch but good."

I raise an eyebrow, "Say what?"

"I'd give you a hug if I were allowed!" she laughs, "I tell you what; I'll hook you up with double desserts for the rest of your stay here."

"That's okay, Roshawn." I reply.

"Nah, nah... it's already done. Don't you worry none."

"Okay, thanks."

"Hate that little bitch!"

I decide to head back to the room, and try to actually get a few more pages read before lunch time. So, back down the long hallway I trek.

Returning to my bed allowed my current buzz to wear off rather quickly. Once more, I was just a frightened boy, all alone in the hospital. I'm hoping to go home this evening, but I'm not sure what "home" is even going to be anymore. Danielle's all but gone. I've drifted quite far from my family. I'm scared that I'll just wind up having another mental breakdown. I can feel my heart racing. Who do I turn to?

Okay, need to control my breathing.

In, out. In, out. In, out.

Okay, that's a little bit better.

I stand up, and head into the bathroom. It's the only lockable door I've got, and if I'm about to have an anxiety attack... I'd much rather do it in private than put on a show. Just breathe. Maybe brush my teeth. Anything I can do to distract myself... from myself. Come on, lunch time. Hurry up damn it.

It's got to be close to lunch time. I would be able to figure it out myself if they'd put a God damn clock on the mother fucking wall. Okay, Craig... cool it down. Just go back to the foyer.

Heading back down the long hallway, I observe some orderlies rolling a stretcher into Jimmy's room.

"Hey, what's going on?" I ask.

"Just go on about your day, Sir." the thin white orderly demanded.

"Soldier! Is that you?" I can hear Jimmy yelling.

"Yeah, Jim. It's me, man. You okay?" I yell over

the orderly's shoulder.

The heavyset black orderly turns around and firmly puts his hands on my shoulders, "Sir... go on about your day, or you're going to wind up in the hole."

"Get your hands off of me." I say, pulling myself out of his grasp, "Jim, what's up?"

"Soldier! They're makin' me leave." Jimmy yells, "They're takin' out my fuckin' gallbladder."

"It'll be okay, Jimmy!" I yell back.

"Sir, this is your last warning." the white orderly threatens, "One more word out of you, and you're going to time-out!"

I stand there, and silently flip him off.

"That's it! You're outta here!" the black man says, and grabs me by my arm.

"Dude, get your fucking hands off of me." I demand, "I, unlike most of the people here *read* my copy of the patient's bill of rights."

The orderlies look at each other. The black man releases me from his grip.

"You can't fuckin' touch me, man." I state, with a smirk on my face, "There's a scared man in that room, and if by seeing me he gets a bit of comfort... where's the harm in that?"

straitjacket vacation

The orderlies stand in still silence.

The white one finally breaks the silence, "You got five minutes, kid."

The black one follows up with, "Then you're going to time-out!"

"Yeah yeah..."

I walk past the thin white orderly, and bump my shoulder into his as I pass. Jimmy is curled up in his bed, clutching his side.

"Soldier..." he whines.

"Yeah, how ya feeling?"

"Like dog shit... twice removed, son."

"Heh. They're gonna take you to the medical side of the hospital, eh?"

"Yeah. Sure sounds like it."

"You'll be okay." I try to assure him.

"Oh, boy." he winces, "I'm not worried about me. I'm upset I'll be leaving the folks here alone. That I'll be leaving *you* alone."

"We'll all be okay, Jim."

"This place is in your hands now, Soldier." he continues, "I'm counting on you to keep watch over this place."

"I won't disappoint you." I say as I hold up my hand as though I'm saluting him.

"Oh, I know you won't." Jimmy turns his attention to the door, "Okay! I'm ready to go. You cock suckers can take me now."

The orderlies load Jimmy onto the stretcher, and head him towards the Unit's exit.

"Soldier!" he yells one last time before he leaves.

Heading over to the stretcher I answer, "What's up, Jimmy?"

Jimmy removes his glasses, and looks me dead in the eye. He motions for me to come in close. When I get about a foot away from him, he whispers, "Thanks for playing along."

"Wha?"

"Thank you for bein' there for Me." his eyes tear up, "I really do want to adopt you, ya know..."

I smile, "Don't mention it, Jimmy."

He reaches out to me, and shakes my hand. The orderlies wheel him out of the Unit. Roshawn, who had watched the whole episode play out, told me that I was turning out to be a real class act. I thanked her for noticing.

"Boy, don't be so quick to thank me yet." she replies, "Looks like I need to put you in time-out."

Shocked, I turned around to face her, "Time-out? You're fucking kidding me?"

"I'm sorry, Craig." she shook her head, "It's out of my control. The orderlies said it, I need to follow through."

"Whatever." I throw my arms up in the air, "Where is this time-out?"

Lucy and Jean walk by and overhear the conversation.

"Time-Out?" Jean asks, "Craig's gotta go to the hole?"

Lucy scratches her head, "We *have* a hole?"

I turn to face both of them, "Yeah, I'm goin' to the hole."

Roshawn pulls her large body out of her chair, and proceeds to fumble with a prison-guard sized key ring, "Let's go, Weiner!"

I follow her over to what I had originally thought to be a utility closet. She opens the door to reveal a small tight corridor that went on for about twenty feet. At the end of that hallway was another door. Behind *that* door,

was the hole. A tiny room, no larger than a utility closet, with a small water fountain, a toilet and a cot.

"A few hours in here won't kill ya, Weiner." she remarks, "This'll be nothin' for you, ya big super hero."

"Roshawn..." I reply, "And to think. I was just starting to like you..."

"Oh, Weiner... you're breakin' my heart." she laughs, "You'll be in here till at least the end of my shift. So, I'll see ya tomorrow."

"Don't threaten me." I joke.

She laughs as she leaves, closing and locking the door behind her.

I look around my, and take note of my surroundings. The walls have foam rubber type padding on them, held to the wall by small rusted hooks up by the ceiling. The floor is composed of cold cement blocks. The cot I'm sitting on has no pillow nor blankets, not even a bed sheet covering it. The toilet/water fountain combo is rusty steel. There didn't appear to be any water in the toilet, so I'm hoping I don't need to actually use it, not like there's any toilet paper here anyway. I only have a few moments to get used to my surroundings before there's a knock on the door.

"Yeah, come in."

It's the hospital chaplain. He enters with a huge smile cutting through his face. He's holding several

straitjacket vacation

pamphlets and a bible.

"Craig Weiner? Son, can I have a moment of your time?"

"Like I'm goin' anywhere?" I answer, "You got yourself a captive audience right now, padre."

Smiling and puffing out his chest, he continues, "From what the folks up front tell me. You're developing quite the, ahem, following amongst the guests."

"Patients."

"Err, of course."

"I don't have any following, man. I simply speak with a lot of conviction, and that gets to people. Makes them see things for what they really are."

"Err, well... I'd like to talk to you about maybe being a little more... err, discreet about voicing your opinion." he says as he wipes a tremendous amount of sweat from his brow, "It just may help you get out of here quicker. This hospital doesn't allow Sunday releases... however, we may just be able to bend that rule for you. If you play ball."

"A plea bargain?" I snicker, "You're offering me a plea bargain, to get out of the hospital?"

"Err, well... that is to say..." he stammers.

"Ya know what, Dan?" I ask, "It's actually an

attractive offer."

He smiles broadly, "I knew you'd see it our way."

"Well, not so fast." I hold up a finger, "The very fact you want me to be silent, is making me incredibly suspicious as to why."

The smile quickly fades from his face.

"So... no offense, padre." I continue, "But, you can take your deal... and, well... you know."

Tossing the brochures onto the bed, the chaplain leaves the hole.

The brochures he left were from the ministry he runs, and don't appear to be anything worth reading. Only maps to churches and hours of services. Not a whole lot of real reading to do here.

Moments later, there's another knock at the door.

"Yeah... come on in."

A new face enters the room. He's appears to be middle aged, however he's trying really hard to look like he's not. He's wearing a Hawaiian shirt, and khaki shorts. His hair is spiked and frosted, and he's wearing an orange tinged tan, "Mister Craig Weiner!" he exclaims, "It certainly is an honor to finally make your acquaintance!"

"Yeah? Who the hell are you?"

straitjacket vacation

"I'm your social worker. My name is Tad." he gives me phony thumbs up.

"Tad? Your name tag says Theodore... wouldn't that make you Ted?"

"Err, well... I go by Tad!" he's still smiling.

"Okay." I roll my eyes, "What do you want?"

"Oh, nothing. Just to talk. Shoot the breeze, ya know?"

"Heh, I'm surprised you didn't say 'rap'."

"No, I'm not some corny old man." he laughs the phoniest laugh I'd heard in a while, "I'm on the level, man. I'm here for you."

"Oh yeah?" I ask, "Then can you tell me why I'm currently being deprived of my mid-day meal?"

"Um, what?"

"I'm locked in this time-out chamber here, right? It's lunch time, and the patient's bill of rights clearly states--"

His jaw drops, and he begins stuttering, "Well, I think, um..."

"It clearly states that under no circumstances am I to have food kept from me."

"Well, of... of course." he babbles.

"So?" I bob my head from left to right, "I'm thinking we can continue this chat in the day room, while I eat."

"Oh. Yes, Sir. Of course." he replies, "Um, let... let's get going, then."

Following him back out of the hole, I walk with a bit of gravitas in my step. I higher feeling of importance and being. As I'm guided out of the utility closet looking doorway, it appears as though there were quite a few of my peers who had been alerted to my former whereabouts. Looks of compassion are awash on the group... compassion and maybe just a tinge of nosiness.

Tad grabs my lunch tray, and guides me out to the patio. He sends both Alex and Montgomery who were sitting out there back inside. When they leave, he locks the door behind them. He obviously wants to keep whatever we say to each other only between the two of us.

"Mister Weiner." he begins, "I didn't think you'd be a squeaky wheel."

Opening my lunch tray reveals a slimy looking hamburger, and some already cold french fries. I look at my tray, and then at him, "Squeaky wheel?"

"Yes, as in 'The squeaky wheel gets the grease'."

"I'm familiar with the saying, Tad. I'm just trying to figure out how it applies to me."

straitjacket vacation

"Well, there's obviously something you're trying to gain, by being so... up front about your displeasure with the Unit."

"Well." I take a bite of the slimy gray cow meat, "You're wrong on several counts there, Tad."

He's about to speak, but I cut him off, "There's nothing I'm looking to gain here, just the recovery that it's the staff's responsibility to see to it that I get." I take another bite and continue, "And, I'm not displeased with the Unit. I don't like the staff too much, and I don't like a lot of the more condescending policies... well, ya know what? You may actually be right about that one, man. I don't like the Unit."

"What can I do to help you, Craig?"

"That's not for me to say." I wave him off, "It's not my job to run this place."

"Then why are you trying to?"

"You flatter me, Tad. You really do."

"Excuse me?" his nose crinkles.

"I'm not trying to do anything here, man." I choke down a few french fries, "All I'm doing is providing a few acts of kindness for people. If that's what it takes to brighten these folks day... than what's the harm?"

He doesn't immediately respond. Walking over to the patio's cage, he looks at the ground.

"So, back to the hole?" I ask.

"No."

"No?"

"No." he says, in a bit of a firmer tone, "What we're going to do, though... is get you the hell out of here just as quick as possible."

"That's up to my doctor." I smile, "You try calling him and getting his ass in here at a decent enough hour, and I'll blow this jip joint as quick as he gives the word 'go'."

Tad walks over to the glass doors that lead back into the day room. He puts his hands in his pockets, and slowly looks up, "Craig. I'm going to try and appeal to your better judgment."

"Say what?"

"Craig..." he continues, "We have a certain responsibility to all of the guests that stay here, which I'm sure you are well aware of as you are the only guest I can remember that's actually read their bill of rights..."

"It's patients... and yeah?"

"Patients, of course. Anyway, that responsibility is all we have. Once those needs are met... well, that's where things can get a bit... funny."

straitjacket vacation

"Funny?"

"Craig... I'm not sure how much longer you're going to be staying here. What I want you to know is... your stay can wind up being a rather pleasant experience... or, well... a not-so-pleasant one."

"Are you threatening me?"

He laughs, "Of course not, Craig. This is just my final appeal to your... hrmph... better judgment."

"Noted."

He unlocks the door into the day room, and opens the door, "Enjoy the rest of your meal, Mister Weiner."

Several minutes pass before Lucy walks out and joins me on the patio, "What happened to you, Sun Shine?"

I look up from my plate, "Ya know what Lucy? I'm really not sure I should say... I don't want to give you any responsibility for me."

"Okay, then." she replies and stands up, "If you change your mind, you just let me know, son."

"Thanks."

"I'll just leave ya alone for a bit... is that cool?"

"Yeah... thanks."

"I'll keep everyone else inside too, kay?"

"Kay...", and with that I was alone on the patio.

straitjacket vacation

chapter nine
round table revolution

I manage to finish my "meal", and decide to head back to my room to rest a bit, and perhaps use the toilet if my body allows. I walk the gauntlet of the day room, and feel everyone's eyes on me. Stan gives me thumbs up, Jean winks. The girl who looks like Danielle blushes and looks down. Alex is madly blinking his eyes, Victoria or Michelle is eating in the manner you'd usually see a hamster eat. Ginny is passed out on the couch.

Lucy is standing in the doorway, and I ask that she move out of my way. She reluctantly stands down, letting me pass. I drop my now empty tray off in the foyer, and notice that Charlie is being discharged. He extends his hand, and we shake.

Roshawn sarcastically smiles at me, and bobs her head from side to side; I just sigh and shake mine. Down the long hallway and into my room I go.

The rumbling in my stomach informs me that it is in fact time once more to attempt toilet usage. Into the bathroom I go. Another pile of toilet paper is used to line the disgusting seat. Before I sit down, I take a look at myself in the mirror, "One man revolution, Craig. You're about to crash and burn, aren't ya?" I laugh at myself, and proceed to sit down.

An hour later I emerge from the bathroom, having done my business and taken a quick "clean-up" shower. Tad is standing in my doorway.

"Well well well... thought maybe you were swingin' in there."

"No such luck, Tad."

"Oh, I'm only kidding. Your doctor is here."

I nod, and walk past him, down the long hallway, and into the therapy room. Doctor Singh is waiting for me. He's wearing street clothes and sneakers.

"Hey Doc, a bit early today, no?" I smile and extend my hand to shake his.

He stares at me. He's obviously not terribly pleased

straitjacket vacation

with me or with the fact that he's at the hospital right now.

"Everything cool?" I ask.

"You don't look terribly ill."

"Say what?"

"The staff told me you've been complaining of chest congestion nonstop since you took your pills last night. Come now, I've scheduled an X-Ray."

"Whoa, whoa, whoa, Doc." I hold my hands out, "I don't know what you're talking about."

"So, you had no congestion?" he asks.

"I had a bit of *nasal* congestion."

"Why didn't you ask for a decongestant?"

"I did... and Sandy gave me one." I'm growing to be just as annoyed as he is, "Then I went back to sleep."

"Then why did they--?"

I cut him off, "Because they're trying to vilify me to everyone here, I suppose."

"They asked me to have you moved over to the medical side of the hospital... I already put in the request."

"Well, looks like we're gonna have to cancel that,

eh?"

"I... guess so." he scratches his head, "Just *what* is going on here, Craig?"

"Nothin' Doc." I nervously pinch the tip of my nose, "Nothin' you need to worry about."

He has me sit down, and asks me to discuss the day's goings-on's with him. I tell him a bit of what's gone down, leaving out a few details here and there. We do a quick round of meditation, and he prescribes me a new sleeping medication. One that he promises won't congest me. He tells me that although tomorrow is Sunday, he will okay my discharge if he feels I'm ready to go. I thank him, and leave the room.

Roshawn is getting off shift and is passing all her day's information on to a just arrived Sandy. I smile sarcastically at Roshawn, and advise her that she was *this* close to seeing me leave. She pretends to not know what I'm talking about. I give her a "Nice try." and head back down the long hallway to my room.

Stan had just finished taking either his third or fourth shower of the day. He entered our room from the bathroom wearing only his towel. His waist was so small that even one of these undersized hospital towels fit him fine.

He tells me that it's a surprise and a relief to see me, as he'd been advised by the staff that I had an infection in my lung and would be moving over to the medical unit. I tell him that the rumors of my illness

straitjacket vacation

were greatly exaggerated, and I wasn't going anywhere just yet. He smiles, and thanks me for everything I've done for him. He tells me that he has my back if anything "goes down". I thank him.

I hear my name called from behind me. Lucy and Sandy are standing in my doorway.

"Hey, big guy." Sandy greets me, "Sounds like we have had quite the day."

"Something like that, Sandy."

"Craig, what the hell are you thinkin'?" Lucy asks, "You're gonna wind up in such deep shit, boy!"

"Don't worry about it, Luce. Just your average day for a friendly neighborhood psyche ward super hero."

Sandy puts his hand on my shoulder, and tells me to try and lay low for the next few days, if I don't get my discharge as they're his days off. He assures me that as long as he's around, my back is covered, however, he can't make any promises for his off-night staff replacement. I nod, and thank him for all of his help. I say, with great confidence that I'll be leaving tomorrow anyway, so it won't be a problem.

I ask if it would be too much trouble to be left alone for a little while to process the events of the past several hours. Sandy advises me that its visitation hour and I had guests. The time must have gotten away from me; last I knew it was mid-day. I head up to the foyer to find my mother, along with my brother, sister, step-father and brother in law waiting for me.

They are all looking around in total astonishment. I can't figure out why. My mother asks me how I'm feeling, and I tell her I'm doing a bit better. I'm told by everyone that I'm looking well, and I thank them.

I guide them into the day room and the crowd of crazies' parts for us like the Red Sea did for Moses. We head back out to the patio, and sit down for our visit.

"That girl in there looks a lot like Danielle." my mother notes. I agree, and tell her I had to do a double take when I'd first seen her.

I look at my brother, and immediately, feelings of guilt flood my mind. I really wanted to avoid seeing him while I was in here. Any signs of weakness I show in front of him, I feel are detrimental. My sister sits next to me and holds my hand.

"Where *is* Danielle, anyway?" she asks.

"She's..." I pause, "Not able to make it out tonight."

"Oh, is everything okay?" my mother asks.

"Yeah..." I lie, "She just has some family stuff to do today is all."

I could tell that the family knew I was lying. They were too kind to call me on it though. Their eyes became sad, and they began squirming in their seats. I could tell

straitjacket vacation

they were uncomfortable, and were looking forward to this visit being over. To be completely honest, so was I. This resulted in a lot of small talk and general topics of the day that I really had no interest in taking part in. Throughout the hour, several of my new friends popped their heads out to ask how I was doing. Annoyed, I nod and tell them I'm okay.

"Why do they keep asking you if you're okay?" my mother asks.

"I don't know."

"Is everything okay here?"

"Yeah..." I lie again.

"Are you sure? Are they treating you alright?"

"Yeah, ma... everything's cool."

"When do you think you're going to be released?"

"Tomorrow."

"Tomorrow?"

"Yeah... tomorrow."

"Is Danielle going to bring you home?" my sister asks.

"I'm not sure."

round table revolution

We talk a bit more, about my medication and a little more gossip about my peers. About forty-five minutes into the visit, they decide they're going to leave a bit early. I walk them up to the foyer, and notice along the way that Alex is sitting with the girl that looks like Danielle. He looks aggressive and she looks very uncomfortable. I thank them for the visit, and bid them good night.

Heading back into the day room, I sit a table nearby Alex's harassing. The Danielle clone looks at me as if to ask for my help. Once our eyes meet, I nod. Alex is yelling at her about the bible, and the fact that she must be Catholic because she happens to be Hispanic.

"Alex?" I ask, though he continues along with his rant.

"Alex... dude, I got a question." I say, and he kind of torques his head and tightly closes his right eye, as though he hears me, but is trying to block it out.

I lean forward in my chair and snap my fingers in front of his face, "Alex!"

His beady eyes nearly bulge out of his head, "Don't you EVER do that again."

"Calm yourself down, Alex." I lean back in my chair with my hands out, "What are we talking about?"

"This dirty wet-back is a Christ follower."

"Okay." I shrug, "What's so wrong with that?"

straitjacket vacation

"The bible is a book of perversion." he rants, "Stereotypically and logically incorrect passed along as factual. Which on its face, it is absolutely not."

I look at the girl and smirk, "What's wrong with the bible?"

"The bible was written by man. Man is flawed, therefore the book is also."

"Wow, Alex." I laugh, "That *almost* actually made sense."

He's foaming at the mouth again, I'm afraid if he babbles much more that I'll be covered in his frothy spittle.

"Alex... you've read the bible, no?"

He gives me an incredulous look, "Of course I have. I know the book as well as I know the inside of my eyelids."

"Okay--", he cuts me off.

"When my eyes are closed, there is darkness." he rants, "It is only in the darkness where the demons and the devils can come and get you. It is *only* because I am a God Warrior that you are even able to sleep through the night. I fight the demons! I fight the devils! *Every night*, I fight them! I do it for the world, even though none of you deserve it."

He stands up, and shouts "None of you deserve it!!!"

"Alex, cool it man." I try to settle him down. He reluctantly sits back down, "You're upset that people are 'Christ followers', yet, you yourself claim to be a 'God Warrior'. What's up with that?"

"I claim nothing!" he yells.

"Okay man, fair enough." I concede, "Let me ask ya somethin'. What's your interpretation of the bible?"

"It's perverted man words!"

"Do you read it as literal or figurative?"

"I read it for what it is. Silly children's stories."

"Okay... let's say for a second that they are simply children's stories." I continue, "If you lived your life by using the morals provided in these 'stories', don't you think you'd live a good life?"

"I... suppose it would be a possibility."

"Then why not just leave it at that." I ask.

"You're proving yourself to be quite a formidable foil for me." Alex notes.

"Right back at ya, man." I extend my hand, but Alex doesn't shake it. He gets up and leaves the room.

"That was amazing!" the girl states, "Thank you!"

straitjacket vacation

"No problem." I reply, "Please excuse me."

I get up, and head back to the foyer, "Did I somehow miss dinner?" I ask Sandy.

"Yeah, man. Dinner was a bit early tonight... you were in with the Doc."

"Alright." my head sinks, as for the first time since I had been here I am actually quite hungry.

"I'll call down to the kitchen, buddy." Sandy says, "You won't go hungry on my watch."

"Thanks, Sandy."

"Head back into the day room, Craig. I'll bring your tray in when it gets here."

With that, I head back into the day room. I sit at one of the tables, and put my head down.

"Well well well, kiddo." Lucy walks up behind me, "You look as tuckered out as I'd ever seen you."

I lift my head up, slowly and groggily from the table. I see that Lucy is with Jean and Stan. I smile, and cough a small laugh.

"Can we join you?" Jean asks.

"Yeah, sure..."

"Dude, you just totally mind fucked Crazy Alex!" Stan exclaims.

I laugh, "Say what?"

"That mother fucker is ALL fucked up right now." Stan answers.

Lucy chimes in, "He's in his room... screaming."

"Jeez."

I notice the ersatz Danielle sitting by herself playing Solitaire at the next table.

"Excuse me a second, folks." I get up and head over to her table.

Plopping down on the chair across from her, I point at the cards on the table, "Kid, that's gonna be a hard game to win. I don't think they have any full decks here."

She laughs, but I'm sure it's not because of my awful joke.

"What's your story?" I ask.

"Huh?"

"What's your story?"

"My... story?"

"Why. Are. You. Here?"

straitjacket vacation

"Oh, oh... duh, I'm sorry." she smacks herself in the head, "Attempted suicide."

"Oh. Okay, that's too bad."

"I'm Jessica, by the way."

"Oh, cool. Craig." I scratch the back of my head, "You wanna join us at the cool table?"

"Oh, yeah... I'd love to!" and with that, we get up and go to my table.

Sandy brings me my tray of food. The foul odor of the night is chicken soup.

I begin to eat, and we all share our stories. Before I knew it, we were joined by Ginny, Victoria-Michelle and a new woman who introduced herself as Fran. Montgomery was sitting nearby but not in our little group.

Chaplain Dan enters and tries to proceed with the evening faith oriented group. None of the patients even look at him. He tries several times to get our attention, however, by this point I was pretty much conducting a group of my own. A group where everyone had a say, and no one was talked down to. A group where feelings and experiences were shared, and lessons were learned... not where we were told what to think, and how to think it.

"If you're not going to take part in my group, you must all leave the day room!" the Chaplain demanded.

round table revolution

"Okay, Dan." I stand up and head straight out to the patio... alone. I stand in the doorway holding the door open. Jessica cautiously stands up and joins me. Followed by Lucy, Stan and Jean. Rounding out our group is Ginny. As Ginny passes Chaplain Dan she calls him a "Mean old man".

We rejoin our prior conversation, as Chaplain Dan sticks his head out the door. "I guess we're doing this the hard way, Craig?" he asks.

"Padre, I'm doing this my way." I retort, "I can't *make* anybody do anything, just like you can't."

He grimaces his red face and leaves.

We continue our mutual admiration society for the next couple of hours, until it came time to pass out the medication. We reconvened soon thereafter. The after "candy" group consisted of nearly everybody from the Unit, all sitting on the patio sharing feelings and stories. Alex and Montgomery were present, however, not taking part. Alex was frantically flipping through his bible, and Montgomery was simply staring into space as it seems he is apt to do.

They tell me that my new sleeping medication is "the one with the butterfly", and it does a great job of making me incredibly dizzy within the first five minutes of having taken it, however, as far as my level of tiredness is concerned, nothing.

The topic of conversation somehow turns to me.

straitjacket vacation

"Ya know, Craig." Ginny says, "I'm sure you'll be out of here soon, and God damn it, we're going to miss you."

I feel my face blush.

"Yeah, you've been like all of our protectors." Lucy adds, "It's sure gonna be strange when you're gone."

I smile. I can feel my right eyelid get heavy with a mix of dizziness and a dash of exhaustion.

"We definitely gotta get together!" Jean exclaims.

My chin juts into my chest; I wasn't quite prepared for that one. I hadn't yet thought that... eventually, everyone here is going to go home. We're sharing these few moments of time, but, soon we're all going to be alone again. All of our "vacations from reality" are coming to an end, and life will restart.

I debate whether or not I'd like to keep contact with any of these people. Is this an event in my life that I'd like to be reminded of time after time? Are these faces that I'd like to see outside these prison walls? Do I want to play super hero on the outside too? Do I have the capability, heart and mind, to care for these people, and help them solve their problems? More importantly, do I have it in me to deal with the fact that they probably won't need me to.

"Yeah... for sure." I blurt out, only to ensure I don't hurt anyone's feelings.

"You totally saved my ass in there." Jessica says, "I

hope I get out of here before you."

I quietly laugh, she whispers in my ear, "Maybe we can just swap email addresses to keep in touch. Seems like that'll be a bit less uncomfortable."

Still laughing a bit, I nod.

Staring before me, I see the strangest juxtaposition. All these folks that I'd won over, in less than two days. At the same time, part of me wanted to cut ties with these people immediately. All these women, from all walks of life... are sitting here, because of me and my one man revolution.

Fran has been carrying around a small black and white notebook that apparently the hospital had given her (and was supposed to hand out to all patients, so that they could make any notes about their progress). She told us all that she wanted our contact information, as she wanted to put together a reunion of sorts several months down the road. Everybody thought it was a great idea. I did too, to a point. Having this get-together looming on the ever present horizon would imbue me with the responsibility of actually showing up, and having to relive this odd period of my life over again.

We all gave her our addresses and phone numbers, which unfortunately led to a mass information exchange. Suddenly everyone left to their rooms, and returned with black and white notebooks of their own. Everybody wanted my phone number. I had just given my number to Fran, so I couldn't give these people a fake one. I also wasn't in any kind of position to refuse, felt too guilty and for

straitjacket vacation

whatever reason... responsible for the continued well being of these folks.

 I attempted to excuse myself for the evening, but not before everyone gave me their notebooks for me to leave a message in. With a stack of notebooks, I stumble back inside. Holding the day room door open incase anyone else was going to join me in calling it a day. No one followed; too content were they to continue the evening pow-wow. Closing the door behind me, I begin to beam with pride. It seems maybe I brought a little bit of happiness to these people's lives.

 Passing through the foyer, I bid Sandy a good night. Sandy stops me.

 "Craig, ya got a second?"

 "Sure, Sandy... what's goin' on?"

 "I want to level with you." he continued, "You're making a real difference to the people here, but, you really need to consider just backing off a little bit."

 "Again with this, man?" I ask, "Sandy. I respect the hell out of you, honest, I do."

 "I appreciate that, Craig."

 "Yeah, but... I'm gonna do what I'm gonna do." I say, "Right now, I'm just lookin' forward to getting out of here. It was nice knowin' ya, man."

 "Yeah." Sandy replies, "You too, Craig. Good night."

round table revolution

We shake each other's hands, and I head down the long hallway to retire for the evening.

I make it about halfway down the long hallway before I can hear the blood curling vomitous heaves of Stan. I look down, shake my head and carry on. Arriving back to the room, I see that Stan is taking yet another "shower". There's no light coming from the crease under the bathroom door, I figure he'd shoved some towels down there to try to keep the sound in.

I take my slippers off, and climb into bed. Still fully dressed from the day, I pick up the stack of notebooks that were given to me to sign. First one was Ginny's. It was decorated with bright spongy letters and pictures of flowers that were clipped out of magazines. I guess there's an "arts and crafts" group here.

Flipping through her book, I see all of the yearbook like notes that patients past and present had left for her. All quite touching in their own way. I notice Stan smuggled a pencil in the room, I shout "Stan. Usin' your pencil, man!"

In between heaves, I hear a "That's cool, man." Into the middle of Ginny's book I go.

Ginny,

It's strange the way life works out. If even three days ago, anybody on this planet would have told me that I'd be in this hospital, I would have told them that THEY were crazy. I came into this place unwilling to open my

straitjacket vacation

eyes, mind or heart to myself or anyone else in this place. Blaming everyone else for my own weaknesses, and not taking any of the responsibilities for my own.

Yours were the first kind eyes I had seen in this place, and it's not something I'll ever forget. Between your eyes and your words, I could immediately tell that your heart was large and true. You took a terribly frightening and uncomfortable time in my life, and almost completely turned it around for me.

I'd like to thank you for everything, and wish you the very best in everything you do. You deserve nothing but the best. I hope that when you look back on this experience you remember me and your interactions with me fondly.

With best wishes,
Craig

Suddenly, my eyelids become heavy. Knowing that I'll be leaving tomorrow, I'd like to get more of these books signed. Victoria-Michelle's is next.

To Whom It May Concern,

Innocence is something with limitless value. Recently I had gone on a quest to pursue my former innocence... only to find that it's gone forever.

Every day we become just a little more jaded. Every day we lose a touch of our innocence. No matter how many old haunts we visit, or how many times we try to return "home".

round table revolution

Home in and of itself is only what you make of it. It cannot be defined by bricks and mortar, or even... to an extent the people behind it... it's a cliché, I know... but home is only where your heart is.

Keep smiling, and remember that your family... though they may be far away, are always there.

Best,
Craig

I still had to fill out Fran's, Jean's, Jessica's and Lucy's. Realizing that I'm currently losing my coherence, I figure I'll just sign those before my discharge. I pile the notebooks on my nightstand, and lean back in the bed. I take a deep breath, simply to ensure that I could... no congestion tonight. I turn off the light, and fall asleep to the sound of Stan tearing up his throat, and the running shower.

straitjacket vacation

chapter ten
rude awakening

"What the fuck are you doin' in my bed?"

Clenched fists, I shoot up out of bed, "What the fuck?"

Jack was back, and in, at the moment, Stan's face, "Get the fuck outta my bed, ya fuckin' crack head!"

"Craig, what's this?" Stan cries.

"Jack, calm the fuck down!" I shout.

"Nah... Nah... Nah, man." Jack's pacing and waving his finger, "This mother fucker is in my God damn bed!"

"It ain't your bed, man." I try to reason, "You got discharged!"

"Well, I'm fuckin' back, honky-Craig... tell your honky-crack head friend here to get the fuck out of my bed!"

"Jack..."

"Nah... Nah..." he walks over to Stan, "Do. You. Understand. Me? Get the fuck out!"

Stan looks at me.

"Jack, leave the kid alone."

"You gonna make me?"

"Jack. Leave the kid alone."

"Remove me, cracker."

"Okay, Jack. Do. You. Understand. Me? Leave the kid alone."

"Fuck you!"

I laugh, which isn't making Jack feel any better about the situation.

"This is fuckin' funny to you?"

"Yeah, man. You got that whole militant black guy

straitjacket vacation

act down to a science."

"Act?"

"Yeah... act." I continue, "Fuck, man. You can't even take care of your own life... this is, what, your fourth visit here?"

Stan begins to laugh.

"Shut up, Stan." I warn him, "You shouldn't even be here to begin with."

I continue, "Jack... you just head up to the front."

"Or else what?"

"Or else, nothin' man." I shrug, "Because you ain't gonna do a fuckin' thing to me or the kid."

Jack walks up to me, and pushes his nose into mine, "You are a mother fuckin' piece of shit!"

I simply smile. Jacks turns and storms out of the room. Stan thanks me, but I wave him off. I can see the sun is just barely peeking through the blinds.

"It's fucking morning already?" I mutter. Like a zombie, I step into my slippers and wander down the hallway to the foyer coffee pot.

The pill lady is manning the counter this morning. She sarcastically greets me as I pour my first cup. Waiting until I'm just about to take a sip, she stops me to

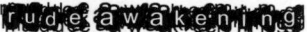

get my vitals, before I "go off and get all caffeinated". I roll my eyes and begrudgingly sit down next to the blood pressure cuff.

As my vitals are being taken, Stan heads towards me. He's literally draped in the sheets from his bed. "Craig, man." he says, "I really really want to thank you!"

"Yeah... it's cool man."

"Hey, uh..." he pauses, "Are you really gonna be leaving today?"

"Good God willing I am." I reply.

"Shit, man... That's really gonna suck. I mean, you're cool as fuck, man."

Taking a sip out of my coffee much to the chagrin of the pill lady, I reply, "Stan, you'll be fine."

He shrugs his shoulders and heads back down the hallway.

"Seems we've got quite the little fan club, huh?" the pill lady notes.

"Something like that." I turn to look at her, "My leaving wouldn't be any big deal at all if any of the patients thought the staff here would help them."

"We *do* help them!"

"Yeah, maybe." I take another sip, "But, you treat

straitjacket vacation

them like shit when ya do."

She looks almost insulted. Which is the emotion I was trying to evoke. Maybe if these people start feeling a shred or two of guilt, they'll actually begin to change the way they look at the patients. "Your vitals are okay, Craig." she says as she removes the cuff.

I shrug and stand up. I decide to join Lucy in the day room. She appears to be in a better mood than usual.

"Hey, you seem happy. What's up?"

"Didn't you hear? Jean's leaving today!"

"No, I hadn't heard. I thought you and Jean were tight?" I pause, "And I thought there were no discharges on Sundays?"

"Hey, hon, I'm not gonna ask any questions... if they wanna kick her skanky ass out to the curb, I don't care *what* day it is."

"You guys always seem like you're cool when you're hanging out?"

"Oh, Craig. I just deal with her, cuz she's here." she shakes her head, "The bitch is nothin' but a no good whore."

"Whoa..."

"She ever tell you why she slit her wrists?"

"Um, no..."

"That cunt was fuckin' her husband's son." her voice lowers to a hushed whisper, "And, he told her he was cuttin' her off... so, she cut her wrists."

"Wow, that's pretty messed up." I reply. I suddenly flash back to the reason why Lucy's currently here, and her sudden animosity begins making a whole lot more sense. I can tell Lucy notices that I just made the connection, as she raises both of her eyebrows, nods and gives me an "uh huh".

"Ah! Mister. Craig. Weiner!" I hear a voice booming behind me.

I turn around, and see that it's Social Worker Tad providing the greeting, "Tad, ain't it a bit early for this?"

"No, sir." he's smiling like the Cheshire cat, "Especially when it has to do with something this serious."

"What, am I released?"

His smile grows even broader, "No Mister. Weiner. Quite the opposite in fact."

"What's going on, Tad?"

"Well, I was kind of hoping you could tell me." he's now standing right in front of me, "The desk was given an anonymous tip about your little drug surplus."

straitjacket vacation

I stand up, "What the fuck are you talking about?"

Holding his hands up, "Ah, ah, ah... Calm down, Mister Weiner."

"Fuck you, Tad."

He's so giddy that he's holding back tears, "Right now, we're going to go to your room. Then... you're going to have some explaining to do..."

He looks away, and then looks right into my eyes, "To the Police!"

"The Police?" I reply, shell shocked.

"Now, let's go." he motions to the same two orderlies I had a run in with yesterday, who come over to me and stand on either side.

We head straight down the long hallway to my room. Upon entry, I see my belongings haphazardly thrown all about the room. Both drawers from my nightstand were removed and turned upside down on my bed. Pages were torn out of my book. My friend's notebooks were all wrecked. My toiletries were emptied all over the floor. In the bathroom, I see that all my mouthwash had been poured down the drain, along with my toothpaste and shampoo. My deodorant stick was crumbled all over the bathroom floor.

"What the fuck is going on here, Tad?" I ask.

He balls up his fists, "Save it for the police, Craig."

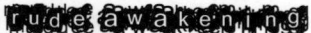

With that, I was forcibly sat down on the floor. Each orderly put a hand on my shoulder to ensure that I remained seated. What feels like an eternity passes before an officer arrives. He's an older man with a thick white mustache who came wafting in with the scent of a stale Swisher Sweet cigar.

"I was told that we have some drug theft?" he asks.

Before I can say anything, Tad rises from off my bed and tries to say that I've been hoarding pills.

"Hoarding pills?" I say, "I have no idea what you're talking about."

Tad begins to laugh, as he reaches into his pocket. He pulls out a plastic sandwich bag that has a good dozen green and yellow pills in it, "Mister Weiner, please explain why we found *this* in your nightstand!"

I smirk, "Shit, Tad. If I didn't know any better, I'd say because you put them there."

"You think this is funny?" the Officer asks me.

"No, of course not." I reply, "This is just another way that the folks behind the counter are trying to ruin my day."

The Officer raises an eyebrow. Tad begins to whisper something in his ear. After a few moments, the Officer knowingly nods.

straitjacket vacation

He drops down to one knee so that he is eye level with me, "Son, everything will be okay."

I furrow my brow, "Excuse me?"

"Oh, your Social Worker tells me that you're going through a real hard time right now. What do you say we just write you up a little warning, and you pay a small fine for all of this?"

"What?"

"No jail-time, this time... okay." he tips his hat, like an old-time police officer would when greeting a lady, "You just stick to the straight and narrow from this point on. Got it, Son?"

"Officer, you've got it all wrong." I plead.

The Officer looks at Tad, and nods. "You take care of this young fellow, will ya Tad?"

"Of course." Tad replies.

The Officer looks back at me, and rustles my hair, "You take care too, Son."

I just stare at him, astounded as he stands back up and leaves.

I too stand up. I begin pacing the floor. Tad stands there nervously, until I finally just get in his face, "Tad. You're a piece of shit."

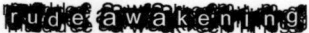

"Hey, Craig. You and I may not be friends, but it's my duty to bring these sorts of situations to the attention of the authorities. It doesn't matter *who* was hiding these pills, I'd have to report it."

"Tad. Those pills aren't mine." I firmly state, "*You* put them there."

"No, Craig... I didn't." he holds his hands up, "I know my word isn't too strong with you, but... seriously, Craig. You have my word on this."

He slowly backs out the door, "I'll... uh, leave you to... uh, clean up your room."

I plop down onto my bed, and start to go through my belongings. Looking at everything I have with my strewn all over the room almost makes me tear up. I just look around in disgust.

"Fuck it." I say aloud to myself.

I head into the bathroom to gather my thoughts, and to put myself behind the only lockable door I currently have. I place both hands on the counter and give myself a good look in the mirror. I can feel that the counter is a bit damp under my left hand. I lift up my hand to find a yellowish-green sludge on my palm.

"Stan."

It's suddenly clear who planted the pills.

"Fucking Stan."

straitjacket vacation

What did I ever do to Stan to deserve this?

After composing myself and washing my hand I head back down the long hallway. It appears as though I'd missed breakfast due to my apparent indictment. I'm greeted by several patients along the way, though I ignore them all. Sights set on Stan, I head straight for his couch in the day room.

I stand before him, and look him in the eyes. He's fidgeting with his tongue amongst his lower teeth, looking as though he has a wad of chewing tobacco wedged in there. I don't even have to say a word, and he stands up.

I widen my eyes, and he turns to leave the dayroom. I follow him all the way down the long hallway and back to our room.

He turns around to me and says, "Dude, it's so fucked up what that bitch Tad did to you man!"

Without any emotion, I tell him "In the bathroom."

"What?"

"In the fucking bathroom, Stan."

"Um... Craig?" he begins to shake, "Is everything okay man? You don't look right..."

"Get your ass in the bathroom." I point to the bathroom, "NOW!"

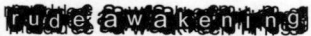

He hustles into the bathroom. I immediately follow, and lock the door behind us.

"Why'd ya do it?" I calmly ask.

"Do what?"

"Don't bull shit me, Stan." I hold up my index finger, "Why did you it? What did I ever do to you, to deserve this?"

"Dude, I don't know what--"

I cut him off, "Stan. Tell me. NOW!"

"Dude, I..." he pauses, "I'm sorry."

I push him into the wall, and push my forearm into his throat, "I've covered for your junky ass this whole time, and you fuck me over like this???"

"I... didn't want you to leave..."

"Stan... you're on your own, man." I let him go, and he slumps to the floor.

I turn off the lights and walk out of the bathroom, leaving Stan in a heap. I can hear him starting to cry. I feel a bit guilty, though I can't let him know that. I figure the best thing for me to do is head back to the foyer and await my discharge.

Upon arrival in the foyer, I run almost head first in to Jessica.

straitjacket vacation

"Whoa, excuse me." I say.

She blushes, and looks down. She hustles around me and heads down the hall to her room.

I follow her down the hall with my eyes, and nod when she turns around to look at me before she enters her room.

"See somethin' ya like?" Jean sneaks up behind me.

"Hey, Jean." I reply, "There's something very familiar about that girl."

"Yeah, she looks like that chickie that came to visit you the other day... your wife?"

"Girlfriend... ex-girlfriend actually."

"Sorry to hear that." she begins rubbing my back. I pull away a bit.

"Hey, I won't bite!" she laughs, playing insulted, "I won't even drag my teeth." she winks.

I roll my eyes, "Hey, best of luck to ya out there."

"Hey, don't think you're gonna get rid of me that easily." she grabs my arm, "I thought we were gonna get together on the outside."

"Well, people always say stuff like that..." I try to reason, "It's like when ya graduate from high school, and you say you'll be best friends forever with all your

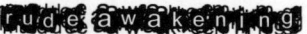

buddies."

She bites her bottom lip, "Well... I know you've got a big house all to yourself right now, don't ya?"

"Yeah... why?"

"Well... I was thinkin' maybe I could... ya know, move in with you?"

"Say what?"

"I'll even, ya know... pay rent."

"Jean, I'm sorry... I ain't interested."

"No, you don't understand." she winks, "I'll... ahem, pay... rent."

"It's cool, Jean... but, I think I'm just going to try to sell it."

"Craig, I'll suck your--"

I cut her off, holding up both hands, "Whoa! That's enough, Jean."

She laughs, "You're no fun."

I sigh, "I guess not. Like I said, best of luck on the outside."

"Yeah yeah yeah..."

straitjacket vacation

I head into the phone area to try calling Danielle. Although our affections are entirely in question at the moment, I still feel a tremendous amount of guilt for even giving a second look to Jessica.

I slowly dial unsure of what to even say.

"Hello?"

"Hey, babe."

She firmly replies, "What?"

"I, uh... just wanted to talk to you..."

"Well, you can save it. I'll be coming to see you today."

"Really? That's great!"

There's a slight pause, "You're not going to think so after I get there..."

I can't think of what to say, but I suddenly feel completely justified in my earlier wandering eyes.

"I'll see you later." she says before hanging up.

I hang up the phone, and just sit, staring at the phone on the wall. Jessica wanders by.

"Craig?" he says, "Is everything okay?"

"Huh?" I turn around to look at her, "Yeah... kid,

everything's cool."

"Cut it out with the 'kid' stuff, Craig." she giggles.

"Alright, you got it."

"Join me for a coffee?" she asks, "I'll buy."

"Yeah, sure."

"I'm sorry, that was so lame." she blushes.

I smile, "Nah, it's cool..."

She guides me over to the coffee pot, and proceeds to pour me a cup, "Cream and sugar?"

"Yeah... thanks."

We head into the day room, and sit on the couch. It's simply amazing how much this girl resembles my Danielle. It's almost as though I'm sitting here *with* Danielle, the way we *used* to be. Without the years that had jaded us. Without all of the bad times, and the lies… back when we were no more than a couple of twenty-something children, playing with our toys in a vast limitless world. Back in those days, all we needed to do was *see* each other to have the perfect day.

Deep in this girl's eyes was the naïveté that I feel I had stolen from Danielle so many years ago. So much wonderment, such passion... the type someone would have to be blessed to have experienced once, let alone twice.

straitjacket vacation

"So, uh Craig... what do you do for fun?"

For fun? This is beginning to feel like we're on a first date, "Um, I like to read, and write... not too much time for anything else, what with being crazy and all."

We both laugh.

"How about you? What do you do for fun?"

"Oh, I love to listen to music, and watch movies... ya know, regular stuff."

"Cool. Hope ya don't mind me askin'... but why'd ya try to kill yourself?"

"Whoa, you don't beat around the bush, do ya?"

"Not my style, kid... err, Jess."

"Well... since you asked so kindly." she bats her eyes, "I tried to kill myself because I'm having trouble with my emotions."

I take a sip of my coffee, "Sounds to me like you're side-stepping the question, Jess."

"Okay... first you tell me why you're here." she answers with a bit of confidence on her face.

"I have extreme anxiety attacks."

She blinks quickly, "Oh... that's it?"

"That's it."

"Oh..."

"Yeah... your turn."

She laughs, "I'll tell you later... maybe."

I smile, "Okay."

I notice Lucy entering the day room.

"Hey, Craig... what's this, ya cheatin' on me?" she jokes, "And with a younger woman?"

I laugh, "Nah, of course not, Luce."

She walks over and pats me on my knee, "Heard you had a run in with the law..."

"Yeah, sure did." I answer.

"Stan told me all about what went down, he's really sorry."

"Stan..." I lean in close to Lucy, "... can go fuck himself."

"Oh, Craig." she tries to calm me down, "He's just a scared kid... tsk, you're gonna do the right thing in the end. I shouldn't be worried."

"I think I already _did_ the right thing, Luce."

straitjacket vacation

"Oh, Craig." she shakes her head, "Choking the poor boy out?"

Jessica's eyes widen, "Wait, what am I missing here? You choked out Stan? Why?"

Lucy and I tell Jessica the story of my recent run in with the police, and she grabs my hand. She gushes over how much I must mean to Stan for him to do that to try to keep me here. Knowing I wasn't going to be able to get *my* anger and point across, I only shrug my shoulders. These two are far too convinced that what happened was a thing I should feel honored by and not angered by.

Lucy taps me on my knee again, "Oh! Craig, you should've seen it!"

I look at her inquisitively.

"While you were fightin' Johnny Law, we had our morning meeting." she explains, "When it came to the point where we all make our daily goals..."

"Yeah?"

"Everyone had *their own* goal!" she smacks my knee, "You would've been so proud!"

"That's great, Lucy." I say, "That's what these folks need. *Real* goals... Goals of their own... Something to work towards *besides* their various mental disorders."

Something I've began feeling very strongly about was

not letting yourself become defined by your various mental illnesses. I feel that the first step towards getting your life back to normal, is making your illness take up as little of your every day as possible, while still keeping it in check. It seems as though the folks on staff around here want to make it so your entire life will, from this point on, revolves around the reason you were originally admitted.

    Out of the corner of my eye, I see Doctor Singh. I excuse myself to see check with him on the status of my discharge.

    "Hey, Doc!" I wave to him, he has an uncomfortable look on his face.

    "Craig." he nods at me, "How are we today?"

    "Um, *we're* fine, Doc... uh, what's the matter?"

    "I'm sorry, Craig." he cracks his knuckles, "I wasn't able to get your release finalized for today."

    "Say what?"

    "Yes, I'm afraid... in light of, well, recent *findings* in your room. They want to check your blood."

    "Doc, ya gotta believe me... those pills weren't mine." I plead.

    "Craig, I'd really like to believe you." his head shrugs into his body, "But, you must understand that the hospital has certain protocol they need to follow through with in these circumstances. Could be a few more days."

"Yeah, Doc. Whatever." I turn, and head back towards the day room.

"Craig." he stops me, "How was last night? Your new medication?"

"It was fine, man." I look back at him over my shoulder, "Doc, I really think I'm ready to go home."

"I'm really sorry, Craig." he replies, "You have another appointment with the medical doctor today. He's going to give you a good once over."

"Yeah, swell."

Back in the day room, it appears as though Lucy and Jessica are becoming better acquainted. They've been joined by Fran.

I throw my hands up in the air, "Good news, everybody!"

"You're outta here, huh?" Lucy answers.

"Nope. I'm stuck in this shit hole for at least a few more days!"

"What?" Jessica asks, "How can they do that to you?"

"Because." I hold up a finger, "I'm on drugs!"

"Wow, that *really* happened?" Fran asks.

"Sure did."

"I thought the staff was making that up to scare us."

"Nah, no such luck there." I pick up my coffee cup, "I'll talk to you all later on."

I head out to the caged patio and see that Jack and Alex are both sitting out there.

"Well, look who the fuck it is..." Jack greets me. He's sitting at the far patio table and he's cracking his knuckles, "You don't look all that tough right now."

"Jack." I pause, "Fuck off, man. I'm not in the mood."

He stands up to approach me, muttering about how "we ain't done yet". I ready myself for a fight. Alex stands up, and I'm unsure whose side he is going to be on... if anybody's. Alex stares at me with almost sad eyes. Jack continues his approach.

"I'm gonna fuck you up, you white faggot!"

The patio door opens, and Tad exits the dayroom. I'm sure he's going to break this fracas up before it escalates to ugly proportions. He looks at Jack, who immediately backs down. He then looks at Alex, who walks past him and back in to the dayroom. Then finally, he looks at me. He smiles, and then looks back at Jack.

He pulls the day room drapes closed, and stands guard

at the door, "Craig." he says with a sick smile on his face, "This just isn't your day."

Jack restarts his approach across the patio floor. He's dancing like a prize fighter, ready to knock out his latest victim, "You want the first punch, faggot?"

"Jack." I reply, "I'm not interested in fighting you."

"Nah, nah... you don't got that choice any more."

"Dude, just calm down." I try to reason, "There's no reason for us to be fighting."

"You think you can try to punk me out, and not have me take a piece out of your ass?" he laughs, "You one dumb fuckin' honky."

He gets in real close to me, "Last chance for your first punch."

"Jack." I look down, "Just go ahead and hit me... so we can end this."

"Nah... you hit me."

"Jack, I ain't gonna hit ya."

"Hit me faggot!"

I smile, and shake my head. He gets right in my face, pushing my nose with his. He's snorting and snarling, and his breath is rather unpleasant. His

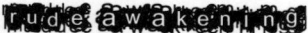

yellowish eyes are nearly bulging out of his head.

"Are we done?" I ask.

He turns away from me, then suddenly turns and swings at me with the wildest punch I ever recall seeing. I easily dodge the punch, which actually came closer to landing on Tad than it did me. Out of pure instinct I lurched back a bit and accidentally tossed my hot coffee at him.

"Ow! Mother fucker!" Jack drops to the ground.

"Shit, Jack." I kneel down to attend to him, "I'm sorry, man."

"Craig." Tad grabs me by the shoulder, "Just get inside."

I walk past Tad, and open the day room door. Before I go inside, I turn to Tad and smile, "Didn't work out the way you thought it would, eh?"

He doesn't even reply. Instead, he kneels down in front of Jack to ensure he's okay.

Upon reentry I'm greeted by my small group. They all seem to know exactly what was going on out on the patio.

"Are you okay, hon?" Lucy asks.

"Yeah, not a scratch on me..." I reply.

"What happened?" Jessica asks.

straitjacket vacation

"He threw a punch." I begin to chuckle, "And I threw my coffee."

"You did not!" Lucy says, shocked.

"The hell I didn't." I laugh, I continue on my way through the day room, up to the foyer where I ask the just having arrived Roshawn when the medical doctor would be in.

"Son, I just walked in the God damn door... you ask me stupid shit like this?"

"Never mind." I roll my eyes, "Just come and get me when he gets here." I walk away and I can hear her ranting about how she's not my servant, and how I have no right to tell her what to do. When I get about halfway down the long hallway, I shout "Are you still talking?" for which I'm called a "little bastard".

chapter eleven
the home stretch

Back in the room, Stan is in the shower again. I set about gathering my belongings that had been tossed around during the room search. I take special care in picking up the other patient's notebooks, making sure that all of the pages were in the right books. The very fact that pages were torn out in the first place during the search was odd, and I figured the reasoning was beyond me.

I fold my clothes and place them back in my nightstand, and throw all the scattered and destroyed toiletries in the garbage. I climb up into my bed, and proceed to wait. Waiting for something I'm not even sure is coming. Waiting.

straitjacket vacation

Lucy and Jessica had slowly followed me back to my room. I almost felt their eyes on me for my entire journey down the long hallway. Now, both were standing in my door way with sad looks on their faces.

"Hey, hon." Lucy says, "It's group time. You comin'?"

"No."

"Oh, come on, Craig." Jessica pleads, "Group won't be the same without you."

"Yeah." Lucy adds, "We get to go to the other side today."

"The other side", there are two sides to The Unit; one was for the more non-violent crazies such as us. The other side, however, was full of criminals and violent crazies.

"The other side, eh?" I smirk, "Yeah. I think I wanna see that."

I get up and pound on the bathroom door, "Stan, quit snortin' that shit and get out here. We got a group."

Within seconds the bathroom door flies open, and Stan leaps out and embraces me, "Ya mean it? We're goin' to group together?"

I push him off of me, but can't help smiling just a little bit, "Yeah, jackass. I don't forgive ya, but, I'm willing to be civil."

Jessica and Lucy give us an "Awww." that I wave off, sarcastically.

The four of us head back down the long hallway, past the foyer, and wait at the large steel door. A lot of our fellow patients are also waiting. Roshawn waddles her rotund hind-quarters over to the door, and manually unlocks it.

We're all guided across the entranceway and into the famed "other side".

The other side is not terribly different than ours. Architecturally, it's the mirror opposite. The opposite foyer, the opposite day room, and the opposite long hallway leading down to the rooms were among the sights. This side had a much more childish, almost "kiddie" feel to it. There were small children's picnic tables in the foyer and down the long hallway adorned with tattered coloring books and used-up crayons on them. There were pages that had been torn out of the coloring books taped to the walls. The smell was an odd stale sweet. Like the smell of a pillowcase filled with Halloween candy found the following summer.

We were herded into the other day room, and we all took our seats. My little group stayed to itself. The citizens of the violent side, for the most part, looked rather normal. Though, there was one who was ranting about killing and disemboweling his wife, and choking his father-in-law with the insides of his wife. Lucy pats me on my hand, sending a message for me not to comment. I cough out a small chuckle, as I was amazed she could read my mind so

straitjacket vacation

well.

This group was run by Natica. The same girl I had a run-in with last time.

"Hello, children!" she hustles in and mockingly greets us.

After sorting out her papers, she spots Alex sitting in the corner of the day room reading out of his bible, "Okay. You can leave now, Alex."

He looks up, and seems a bit insulted, "Excuse me? I haven't said or done anything."

"Yeah yeah yeah, we'll just call this a bit of preventative maintenance. Buh-bye, Alex." she mockingly waves at him by repeatedly folding her hand.

Alex shrugs and starts to stand up.

"Sit back down, Alex." I say.

"It's cool." Alex says, which almost shocks me, "I'll go."

"No, man." I turn and look at him, "You're staying."

"You need to mind your own business and let him go." Natica says.

I turn my attention back to her, "So. Let me get this straight." I crack my knuckles, "*Our* Alex has to go..." I then point to the wife slaughterer across the

room, "But *their* Alex gets to stay?"

Her eyes widen, and her eyebrows furrow.

"Fuck that, Natica."

She give me a sarcastic smile, "Ya know what? You want to run this group. You got it."

She leaves the day room, and everyone looks at me. I stand up, and lean against the wall, "Did I speak outta turn?" I ask the room. No one answers. I sit back down.

We sit in silence for a few minutes before Natica returns. This time she's wheeling a cart full of craft supplies, "Since I'm not going to be able to do my group, I guess this will be Arts and Crafts." She parks the cart in the middle of the room and leaves.

I grab one of the notebooks off the cart, and leave the room. I go to their counter, where a woman not unlike our own Roshawn sat. I asked to be cleared to go back to our side of the Unit. She buzzed me out without any argument. While crossing between the two sides, I run into Danielle. She's dressed quite well and is carrying an envelope.

"Babe!" I exclaim, and go to hug her. She puts her arms up to stop me.

"What're you doing here this early?" I ask, "Visiting time isn't for a few more hours."

"I know..." she answers.

straitjacket vacation

"What's with the envelope?"

"It's, uh... for you." she replies.

"Weiner!" Roshawn yells, "Get your skinny butt back in here. You know the rules."

"Yeah, gimme a minute here, Roshawn." I turn my attention back to Danielle, "So, what's in it?"

"You can just read it... later though."

"No, tell me."

"Weiner! Don't make me call the orderlies!" Roshawn again yells.

"Look, you're going to get in trouble. Just read the note later."

"Tell me what's in it!" I demand.

"It's just... I've decided to try and claim the house over to you." she answers, "The forms is in here for you to sign; hopefully you'll be able to qualify on your own. There's also a... well, a note in there from me." she begins to cry.

"I can't believe you're doing this." I say, numb.

She continues to cry as she slowly walks backwards down the corridor to the exit. The orderlies come up behind me, and grab me at my elbows. I don't put up any

sort of struggle or fight as they slowly drag me backwards back into the Unit. The heavier-set black orderly snatches the envelope out of my hand, "We'll have to inspect this. Weiner."

I hear the low hum of the steel door buzz, and the "chin-clud" of the door swinging open. Seconds later, the door swings shut. I sit on the floor just inside the Unit.

"If you is done sulkin', the doctor is here to see you." Roshawn informs me after a few minutes go by.

Great, that asshole. I can't help but chuckle a bit thinking that he's telling himself the same thing about me.

The orderlies return and inform me that they will be escorting me to my doctor visit, as they now perceive me as a potential flight risk. I tell them if they touch me I'll sue the hospital. They both take a step back.

I'm buzzed out of the Unit, and proceed to the same doctor's office that I'd visited several days ago. I walk a few steps ahead of the orderlies, and enter the office before I get invited in.

"Take a seat." the doctor says, not even turning around to greet me. I stay standing until he does.

"Looks like we're taking blood and urine today." he says, "Have you ever been drug tested before?"

"Yeah." I answer, "When I got hired at my job I had to take one."

straitjacket vacation

"Okay." he flips through his chart, "This one's going to be a little bit different than that one."

"Oh yeah?"

"Yeah." he pauses to cough, "If you fail this one, there's a good chance of you getting criminal charges filed against you."

"Swell." I roll my eyes, "It's a damn good thing that I'm sure I'm clean."

The doctor rolls his eyes and gives me a sarcastic "uh huh."

The doctor's demeanor was a bit different today than it was before. He seems both annoyed and amused at the same time, if that makes any sense. I couldn't quite put my finger on it until he asked me to remove my pants. It appears as though I'm expected to urinate into a cup right in front of him, so that he could "ensure the urine is mine". Realizing that seeing me in an uncomfortable situation is what he wanted; I nonchalantly removed my pants, folded them, and placed them on the examination table.

He handed me the cup, and asked me to go ahead. It takes a few moments, but I'm finally able to go. I hand the cup back to him, and put my pants back on.

The little Asian vampire then enters the room with her blood work tray. I stick out my left arm, and look in the other direction.

"Ah, you too funny." she says as she wraps the piece of rubber tubing around my bicep.

A minute or two later, and I'm on my way back to the Unit. My concierge of orderlies accompanies me. Overcome by a sudden burst of weakness, I trudge down the long hallway to my room. It doesn't take me very long to fall asleep.

I wake up as it's beginning to get dark outside. "Perfect." I moan to myself as I shake my head. On my nightstand is the letter from Danielle. I feel incredibly dirty and invaded looking at the envelope that had been haphazardly torn asunder by the staff here. Knowing they read, and probably enjoyed every word of Danielle's farewell address to me only added insult to injury.

I go to pick up the letter, however, decide not to read it just yet. Maybe never read it at all. Reading it will only make it real. I sit up in bed, and look around. The room had been tidied up a little bit. I'm guessing Stan is responsible for that. I crack my neck, and unsuccessfully attempt to crack my tense lower back before getting out of bed.

As I'm about to leave my room, Sandy knocks on my already open door.

"Hey, ya decent?" he jokingly asks covering his eyes.

"Hey, yeah Sandy." I scratch my head, "Thought you were off today?"

"Yeah, I am buddy." he extends his hand, "Just wanted

straitjacket vacation

to wish you well before you go."

"Say what?"

"You're outta here, man!" he exclaims, "Your tests came back negative. You're on your way, pal!"

I grab Sandy in a manly embrace, and lift him off the ground, "This is awesome, Sandy!"

He tells me that there were some strings attached to my release, and I'd have to discuss them with Doctor Singh, but after that, I was a free man.

I thank him again, and excuse myself. I head back down the long hallway, to the foyer, where I ran into Lucy, Jessica and Stan. I give them my news, and they all seem a bit upset, though genuinely happy for me.

In the continued whirlwind of euphoria, Doctor Singh calls me into the therapy room. I quickly comply, and head straight in.

"Please, take a seat Craig." the Doctor says, somberly.

I sit down, though I cannot sit still. My heart is beating out of my chest at the prospect of getting out of here tonight. I'm afraid that I'll be perceived as having an anxiety attack now, just as I'm within "field goal range" of the egress.

"You feel that you are ready to leave?" he asks.

I nod, almost feverishly. Bobbing my head, "uh huh, uh huh."

"Okay." he pushes his glasses up the bridge of his nose, "I must tell you, Craig. I do have some reservations about granting you your release."

"I understand, Doc." I reply, "I'll be back for outpatient though, right?"

"Yes. Yes, you will." he clears his throat; "However, I am more concerned about your health and stability in the more immediate future."

I look down, and the bobbing of my head slowly begins to wane.

"You have family living nearby?" he asks.

"Yeah."

"If it's not too much trouble, and if it's okay with them..." he pauses, "I would like to see you stay with them for the next few weeks."

"Seriously?" I ask.

"Only if it's okay with them and with you. I do not wish to put anybody in a strained or uncomfortable position, you understand."

"Yeah..." I cock my head to the side, "And if I choose not to stay with family?"

straitjacket vacation

He looks at me from above his glasses, "Then, I cannot in good conscience grant you your release at this moment."

"Okay, Doc. I'll call my mother and see if it's cool to stay with her."

He smiles, "Thank you, Craig. I will take you at your word, and grant you your release tomorrow morning."

I smile wide, "So... it's official?"

He smiles back, though he tries not to, "It's official."

chapter twelve
goodbye farewell amen

Heading back into the day room, after hearing about the news of my release was a real guilty pleasure. I felt pretty bad leaving these folks behind, though, I couldn't help but smile.

Jessica and Lucy were sitting on the couch, and Stan had pulled up a couple of chairs. I sat in the empty one, and shared my news. As soon as I'd made it clear that I was leaving in the morning Jessica excused herself to her room. Lucy advises me that Jessica had developed a bit of a crush on me. Stan just sat there, didn't really say much. I can tell he'd just finished taking one of his "showers".

straitjacket vacation

    I scooted over to the couch next to Lucy, and ask her when she thought she'd be getting released. She tells me that this is her third visit to a place like this, and her usual stays are about two weeks long.

    "What time you think you'll be leaving tomorrow?" she asks.

    "I don't know. I figure my mom'll probably pick me up... she'll probably get here pretty early."

    "You think you'll be here for breakfast?"

    "Yeah, probably."

    "Good." she looks down, "We'll say good bye then."

    "Yeah."

    "This place won't be the same without ya."

    I smile, "This is gonna be pretty awkward, ain't it?"

    "Probably..."

    Then, at the same time we both say, "We're probably never gonna see each other again..."

    I continue, "Just like back at high school graduation, eh?"

    "Exactly..." she replies.

    "You think Jess'll come out of her room tonight?" I

ask.

"Eventually she will." Lucy shrugs, "She's a young girl, ya know? You're this brave super hero that's protecting all of us. It's only natural for her to develop a crush."

"I guess." I smile. I stand up to excuse myself, as there were some matters I wanted to attend to before I left, signing people's books as well as scheduling my ride home.

On my way to my room, I stop at the phone area to call my mother. She's quite pleased to hear that I'm released, and she tells me that she'd pick me up early tomorrow morning. I decide not to ask her about my moving in for a little while, as I really didn't want to put anybody out. I also knew that I would use it as a crutch later on down the road.

I head down the long hallway for what may be the final time in the direction of my room. Jessica's door is open; I knock on the door jamb as I walk by and wave. She was face down in her bed, though she did look up when I knocked. She looks incredibly upset, near tears.

As I continue to walk, her meek voice calls out my name. As I turn around to see what she needed, she grabs my hand and squeezes, she's holding a piece of paper she had torn out of her notebook, "If I... give you my number... would you, maybe think about calling me... sometime?"

Torn between my emotions, guilt, and the fact that

this girl so resembled Danielle, I wasn't sure which way to go with this. I decide to take the paper, and tell her I would, as I figured it would be the easiest way to say good bye to her.

She grabs me in an embrace, and begins to cry on my chest. I gently rub her back, and assure her that everything was going to be okay. She looks up to me, and our eyes meet. It was just as though I was looking at Danielle for the very first time. I begin feeling my heart in my throat, as our faces grow ever closer. Her mouth begins to slowly open, and mine cannot help but follow suit. I touch and hold her face with both of my hands as our heads lean to either side. Just before our lips meet, I catch a glimpse of the ring that I still hadn't taken off of my finger.

I pull back, and feel as though I could vomit. My mouth became so full that I cannot even work out an apology. I push her away, and hustle down the long hallway to my room.

The evening passes into night and finally to morning. Seemingly seventy-five hours later, day breaks once more. I spent most of the night unsuccessfully trying to write letters to Lucy, Jessica, and Stan. I would've liked to leave an impact on these three most of all. The sentiment was there, however, the words were not.

As soon as the first ray of daylight peaks into my window, I head down the long hallway for the final time. I was happy to find that I was the first patient to wake up, so that I could make my escape without having to really say good bye to anybody.

goodbye farewell amen

I get up to the counter, and speak with the pill lady in regards to my release. She asks who my pharmacy is, and I tell her that I'd probably be picking up my medication at my local grocery store. She fills my prescription over the Internet, and tells me that it will be ready by the time I get there. She advises me to be very careful with my new sleeping pill, as it's very strong. I would have to self-test to ensure proper dosage. I told her I'd be careful.

She pulls my belt out of my locker and hands it back to me; I place all of my belongings in the same bag.

I pour my final cup of the Unit's terrible coffee and peek into the day room. Stan is passed out on the couch. I walked in and tucked my attempts at farewell notes under his pillow.

I take a few sips of the coffee and toss out the rest.

"I'm ready to go." I inform the pill lady who nods, and buzzes the large steel door.

I take one final look around.

The long hallway doesn't look quite as long anymore, in fact, the entire Unit looks a whole lot smaller.

I grab the large steel door's handle and pull it open.

"Thought you'd get away without saying goodbye?"

straitjacket vacation

Shit.

I turn around to find Lucy leaving her room. I put my head down, and nod the smallest nod I could muster. She slowly walks in my direction, "I guess I understand. I was never good at goodbye's either."

"I'm sorry." I sigh, "I just thought it would be easier this way."

She nods, "We're really going to miss you here."

"Ya know… I may actually kinda miss being here." I laugh.

"Li'l girl told me what happened between the two of ya last night."

"Oh…" I groan, "She did?"

"Yeah." She rustles my hair, "You showed some restraint. You need to go home and work things out with your girlfriend."

I nod.

"Can I get a hug?" she asks.

I laugh, "Of course. Not sure what I'd have done here without you."

"Oh, stop. You'd still have taken over the place." She wipes a tear from my face that I hadn't even realized was there.

"Give the gang my regards."

"I will." She begins to laugh through her tears, "You take care of yourself."

I nod as I head back over to the door. Before opening it, I turn back to find that Lucy had already headed back to her room.

Opening the door, I take a deep breath, and take my first step into freedom. I wander down the hallway that the medical doctor inhabits and out the double doors into the hospital atrium. I sit on a bench, and breathe in my first breaths of my new life.

My mother arrives about two hours later to pick me up, and is quite surprised that I had checked myself out. I just shrug and allow her to guide me to her car.

I get into the passenger seat and stare out the windshield to this vast new world I now lived in. It was a world without walls, or groups, or the long hallway. Also, this was a world where I'm now once more a mere mortal… no longer a super hero. There's nobody for me to save out here, anyone that I had thought counted on me, either proved in my absence that they didn't need me or just plain abandoned me.

"I need to stop at the bank and the post office." my mother tells me, "Is that okay?"

Still staring forward, I nod.

straitjacket vacation

"Oh and here are your keys, wallet and cell phone." she says as she hands me my belongings.

I stare down at them, and my stomach turns. I had almost forgotten about these tiny parts of my life. I think I almost wanted to forget about them completely. I flip open my cell phone, and see that it says I have no service. I figure Danielle must have turned it off.

Driving down these roads that should be familiar is oddly not. I have only been taken out of society for about four days, and yet, the world was now a complete stranger to me.

My mother pulls up to the bank and asks if I'd like to come in. Still staring forward, I shake my head. She tells me she'd be right out.

Across the street is a restaurant where people are hustling and bustling, picking up their breakfasts and brunches. I almost shield my eyes and cower in fear which is scary in and of it. I begin breathing heavily, realizing that I may no longer be able to handle even the most mundane parts of life.

In the center console of my mother's car, I see a bunch of envelopes addressed to me. Various billing statements just happened to arrive in my mailbox while I was gone. I swallow down a hard gulp of heartburn inflamed bile. My mother returns.

"Okay, now the post office." she says, "Are you feeling okay?"

goodbye farewell amen

Still staring straight, almost fixated on the folks at the restaurant across the street, I nod.

We pull up to the local post office and I again choose to wait in the car. Across the street are homes, not too dissimilar to mine. There are people walking their dogs, people checking their mail, people just being people.

It terrified me.

My mother returns several minutes later, "Do you have a prescription to fill?"

"They, uh, filled it at the hospital..." I stammer, "It'll be at the grocery store down the block by the time we get there..."

"Oh, great!" my mother says, "We can swing by their next... maybe pick up some things for a big return dinner for you."

"Oh, okay..."

"Will Danielle be able to come too?"

"I don't think so."

We get to the grocery store, and head to the back where the pharmacy counter is. I give them my name, and they give me my medication. When they ask me to pay, I fidget a bit before handing my mother my wallet. I seemed to have forgotten how it operated.

We begin walking up and down the aisles of the store

straitjacket vacation

looking for what to have for tonight's dinner. My mother asks me what kind of soda I'd like to have... and I... lose it.

I burst into tears. Almost painful heaving tears. My mother grabs me and covers me, and we head for the front door. I'm unable to breathe, and my crying is stifled.

We get back to my mother's car, and I'm able to catch my breath and I sob into my sleeve.

My mother doesn't ask me any questions and instead takes me straight to my house. Pulling up to my home and into the driveway, a lot of old feelings return… a lot of the old weights I'd thought I'd shed were now back on my shoulders. I reenter my house to find my furniture tastefully placed around. My mother and sister had taken the weekend to make my house look more like a home.

In a daze, I sit down at my new dining room table, and stare into the backyard. My mother sits down at my side.

"Do you like it?" she asks.

Not taking my eyes off my backyard, I nod.

"Are you okay?" she asks, "Would you like to maybe stay with us a few days?"

I shake my head and we sit in silence for a few minutes.

I stand up, and begin pacing.

"You sure you're okay?" my mother asks.

"I'm just having some trouble acclimating to life." I answer, "I question the hospital's logic taking a reverse claustrophobe and placing him in very tight quarters for several days before releasing him back into the world without a net."

My mother just sits and allows me to rant.

"How am I supposed to go back to work? Back to my everyday routine?" I rant, in a way that reminds me of Alex, "I, I, I'm all alone again."

"Danielle--"

"Dumped me." I cut her off, "She couldn't handle being with a crazy person she couldn't depend on... and I can't say that I blame her."

"But, the house--"

"She's planning on claiming it over to me in full. I have an application form here she wants me to sign."

"Are you going to?"

"I don't fucking know!" I slam my hand down on the table, "I have no fucking idea, Ma. I haven't the foggiest idea what my place in this world is now... if any."

"I think you should come to the house and stay with us for a few days."

"Yeah... maybe." I reply trying to calm myself down, "Can I be alone for a few minutes? I'll head to the house in a little while."

"Okay." my mother says, picking up her pocketbook and heading to the door.

All alone in the house, I stand at the kitchen sink. I survey the quarter acre of land I now own. Own all by myself. The grass had grown an awful lot in the past four days... I'd have to tend to it soon. Alone.

I look to my right, and see my prescription bottles, some bi-polar medication and my sleepers. Four Bi-Polars and one sleeper per day... I shake my head. The shine from my backyard is almost reflected into my kitchen, leaving me standing in an odd stasis between the inside and outside of my property. It's nearly overwhelming; though I am able to compose myself... just long enough to grab my daily pill case from the junk drawer.

I consider the options before me, and as though by serendipity, I manage to spill the entire contents of my sleeping pill bottle all over the counter. I begin counting them… as they grow… increasingly appetizing.

afterword
Chris Sheehan, 2008

This little book of mine has proven to be a whole lot harder to edit and refine than it ever was to write. It's the kind of thing, where you're writing and reliving moments that are very close (some closer than others) to real-life experiences. It's hard to deny a lot of things when they're staring back at you in black and white. With pictures, you can squint… and make yourself see things in a skewed way. Words don't allow any such luxury.

A small bit of background may be in order. This "novel" was written for the 2007 National Novel Writing Month contest (NaNoWriMo for those in the know), wherein the competitors had to put together a 50,000 word novel in 30 days. That all being said, it should come as no surprise that this here story was written at breakneck speed, leaving me very little time to re-read or reflect on anything that I had wrote.

straitjacket vacation

Upon completion, I naively thought that I could simply take this mess I'd put together, get it published, and live off the royalties that would most definitely be coming my way.

Then…

Then, I decided to READ it.

I made it about five pages in before shutting down my word processing program. It was almost painful to see all of my experiences staring me in the face. "Hearing" the way I spoke, "Seeing" the way I acted. It was all too much. As a matter of fact, as of this writing, I've only been able to make it through the story a handful of times… just many enough so I could edit it… and I doubt if I'll ever read it again.

If you've made it this far, I'm going to assume that you've both read the story portion of this novel as well as the first bit of my rambling "After word"… so, I'm not going to worry about spoiling anything from this point on.

I remember sitting awake at The Unit in the middle of the night. I kept thinking what a fantastic story I would make out of this. Kept thinking over and over again, that this whole mess would ultimately make me rich and famous… I'd sell the movie rights, and from there actually begin to make a living as a writer. Surely, there have got to be MILLIONS of people interested in a story of this magnitude.

I'd somehow convinced myself of both my writing prowess, and just how interesting I am/was as a person. I can't figure out which of the two is more detrimental to my

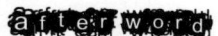

success.

In rereading the heft of this story as recently as today, in my feeble attempt at editing my own work, it is almost absurdly apparent that I've chosen to glaze over certain parts of this story while over writing others.

No one likes to think of themselves as a measure of failures, myself included. I feel I (and the story) would have been better served had I reminded myself more often that Craig isn't me… and that I'm not Craig. Sure, we may share similar experiences, and an acquaintance here and there… but we're by no means the same. Craig's actually about an inch and a half taller than me.

I feel that I had subconsciously chosen to define Craig more by his victories than his defeats. His victories were almost effortless to write, whereas, his failures… were my failures, in most cases… and TERRIBLY difficult to relive in my head, let alone put in print where they'd be there for me to read over and over again.

I'd like to say that I've maybe learned a thing or two from these experiences, but I haven't. I'm still very much the same person as I was before, only now I take a handful of pills each day to ensure my condition doesn't worsen. I keep to myself, and don't really converse nor correspond with anybody.

In closing, at least for now… I'd like to thank anyone that's made it this far with me, and read what, for the most part, is nothing more than an embellished glorified diary entry.

Printed in Great Britain
by Amazon.co.uk, Ltd.,
Marston Gate.